Trapped!

Zel looks around quickly. She sees no door into the tower. This must be the right place, but how will they get in?

Mother's eyes glitter hard in the moonlight. She stares beyond Zel at something.

Zel spins around. The sapling walnut tree beside the tower, which was only half the height of the tower only moments ago, is growing, growing. It thickens and reaches; it grows.

Mother stands and pushes Zel. "Climb. Fast. It is the only way in. Climb!"

Fear strengthens Zel's hands, makes her foothold sure. She goes from one thick branch to another, easily, as though this tree were made to have the branches at just the right distance apart for her legs. One branch leads directly to the wide window ledge of the tower. Zel jumps down inside and turns to help Mother into the room.

Her arms meet empty air. Mother isn't behind her.

"Mother!" Zel climbs back onto the window ledge.

But the walnut branch already retracts. It is too far from the window for Zel to reach.

Zel screams. "Mother!"

The tree is now shrunk to its normal height.

"Mother!"

PUFFIN BOOKS BY DONNA JO NAPOLI

The Bravest Thing
Jimmy, the Pickpocket of the Palace
The Magic Circle
The Prince of the Pond
Shark Shock
Soccer Shock
When the Water Closes Over My Head

Zel

Donna Jo Napoli

PUFFIN BOOKS

PUFFIN BOOKS
Published by the Penguin Group
Penguin Putnam Books for Young Readers, 345 Hudson Street, New York, New York 10014, U.S.A.
Penguin Books Ltd, 27 Wrights Lane, London W8 5TZ, England
Penguin Books Australia Ltd, Ringwood, Victoria, Australia
Penguin Books Canada Ltd, 10 Alcorn Avenue, Toronto, Ontario, Canada M4V 3B2
Penguin Books (N.Z.) Ltd, 182-190 Wairau Road, Auckland 10, New Zealand

Penguin Books Ltd, Registered Offices: Harmondsworth, Middlesex, England

First published in the United States of America by Dutton Children's Books,
a division of Penguin Books USA Inc., 1996
Published by Puffin Books, a member of Penguin Putnam Books for Young Readers, 1998

19 20

THE LIBRARY OF CONGRESS HAS CATALOGED THE DUTTON EDITION AS FOLLOWS:
Napoli, Donna Jo.
Zel/by Donna Jo Napoli.—1st ed.   p.   cm.
Summary: Based on the fairy tale *Rapunzel*, the story is told in alternating chapters from the
point of view of Zel, her mother, and the prince, and delves into the psychological motivations of
the characters.
ISBN 0-525-45612-0 (hc)
[1. Fairy tales. 2. Mothers and daughters—Fiction.] I. Title
PZ8.N127Ze 1996 [Fic]—dc20 96-15135 CIP AC

Puffin Books ISBN 0-14-130116-3

Printed in the United States of America

For Mamma and Marie and Elena and Eva

ACKNOWLEDGMENTS

I thank my family first, for all the time they spent reading and listening and talking about the various versions of this story and for the many wild ways in which they gave criticism and advice. I love them all. And I thank Shannon Allen, Wendy Cholbi, Thad Guyer, Shelagh Johnston, Joel Perwin, Emily Rando, Jennifer Rosenblum, Bob Schachner, Heidrun Taillens, Louise Tilly, and Hansjacob Werlen for comments on earlier drafts. Thanks also go to the American Association of University Women for giving me a summer fellowship in 1995 to visit Switzerland and complete the research for this story.

Finally, and mostly, I thank Lucia Monfried. Acknowledgments can be deceptive because they can suggest help in the form of solid criticisms and strong encouragement. This is not the sum of what Lucia did for me on this story, nor of what she always does for me on stories. Instead, she is my partner—in there working through it all, from beginning to end, over and over and over and over. For this, she has my undying gratitude and love.

Contents

Part 1 • THE GIFT
Switzerland, mid-1500s   *1*

Part 2 • REJECTION   *43*

Part 3 • LONELY   *85*

Part 4 • OBSESSED   *117*

Part 5 • THE KISS   *163*

Part 6 • LOVE   *187*

Part 7 • SCATTERING   *203*

Part 8 • GATHERING   *211*

THE GIFT
Switzerland, mid-1500s

Chapter 1 ❖ Z e l

Oh, Mother, the goose is on her nest again." Zel rests her weight on the windowsill and leans out. Her feet dance on tiptoe. The goose stretches her neck forward and smacks the bottom of her bill on the rocky soil. "Goose!" Zel shouts. "Dear goose. You're terribly confused." Zel hears a thunk. She spins around.

Mother has just put a bowl of apricots on the center of the table. "Forget that goose. Eat well. You'll need your energy."

"I will?" Zel grabs a fruit from the cool water it floats in. She eats greedily, her teeth sharp as the shells she has collected on their visits to the lake. She sees that Mother wears her good shoes. "Oh, we're going to town today!" She laughs. And now her dancing feet take her around the table, around Mother, impelled by the rare joy of town. Zel sings, "Today today today today."

Mother catches the tips of Zel's braids and gives a playful tug. Holding tight, she dips her fingers in the water in the bowl and smooths the curls that have sprung

3

free back into place. Then she turns to the shelf and takes down the dark loaf. She saws with a long, strong knife.

Zel sniffs the air, lifting her nose like the lone chamois she watched one day last month when she climbed high into the Alps. "I love the smell of bread. Sweet, sweet bread."

"Nourishing bread." Mother puts two pieces on the table.

Zel takes a bite of bread, then ties on her shoes. She has already tended to the rabbits and hens, so there is nothing to delay her and Mother. "I wonder if the crier with the melons will be there." She would love to see the crier's wide chest and hear his rough voice.

"The first melons might be ripe already." Mother speaks distractedly.

"Tell me: will he?" Zel chooses a second apricot and rolls it on the table, making a design of its wet trail. She takes hold of her wooden chair by the half-moon hole in its back, pulls it out from under the table, and sits.

Mother smiles. She closes her eyes. When she opens them, she says, "At least a few melons are ripe. He'll be there."

"Mother." Zel's eyes hold Mother's with insistence. "I want to be able to close my eyes and know things, like you. But when I close my eyes, all I do is stumble."

Mother picks up her own hunk of bread. She eats, quick and silent.

Zel stands with her eyes closed and bumbles her way across the room, through the doorway, purposely bumping into baskets and beds. She opens her eyes and laughs. "Let's go."

Mother takes a cloth sack off the peg on the wall. She picks up the piece of bread that Zel has left on the table and slips it in Zel's pocket as she walks past and out the door.

On the side of the next mountain to the east, a herd of long-horned goats skips over stone loosened by spring rains. There is little grass on that mountain, but on Zel's and Mother's meadow the grass is thick as moss. No place on earth is as fine as their alm. Zel skips through the grass, mimicking the goats.

"Keep clean, Zel. We must be presentable for town."

"Everyone else will be caked with grime."

"We aren't everyone else."

Zel doesn't understand Mother's passion for cleanliness. No one else seems to share it. Still, she returns to the path.

"Pay homage to the cypresses." Mother nods toward the row of tall trees.

Zel bows her head. These are the only cypresses Zel has ever seen in all her mountain wanderings. They define the edge of their alm. One winter night the thunder of snow breaking from the mountainside woke Mother and Zel, and by the time they managed to rush

5

from the cottage, the avalanche was over—blocked by the looming trees. Zel was sure the trees had not been there before that night, but Mother said it's easy not to notice trees and plants until you need them. Mother notices every tree everywhere, it seems. Zel has little sense of trees, but gratitude renders her reverent before these cypresses, which seem to grow thicker by the day.

The goose swings her neck and gazes at them. Beyond the goose, the gray tomcat moves in a silent crouch on the bridge. But there's no cause for alarm: The goose isn't unaware; Zel can see that from the angular movements of the goose's head. Rather, the goose is flustered: Which threat is greater, humans who might eat eggs or a tom who attacks birds? In an instant she's made her decision. She spreads her wings and leaps onto the bridge, charging the cat with raucous honks. The tom turns and runs. Foolish cat to have even thought of attacking. No cat is a match for a goose. Still, Zel admires the cat's saucy spirit.

Zel points at the nest and counts. "Five. This year she's got five. Last year it was only four."

The goose now pivots, her wings wide, and charges Zel and Mother. Zel backs away to give the goose wide berth. But Mother pulls Zel behind her and stays on the path. Mother hisses loudly. The goose halts, honks. Mother hisses more fiercely. The goose returns to her nest. Mother crosses the bridge.

Zel feels betrayed by the goose's attack and even more by the goose's obedience to Mother. She looks over her shoulder and calls, "Silly goose. Who'd want to steal your rocks anyway? No matter how long you sit on them, they'll always be rocks."

The goose swings her head dumbly.

Zel is sorry for her words. The goose cannot possibly understand them, but that makes them worse. "What makes her gather rocks, Mother?"

"I don't know, Zel. Probably her mate was killed and she can't give up the instinct for nesting."

"Maybe she had a nest of real eggs once. Maybe a fox attacked and killed them all." Zel shudders. She thinks about her own future family. She will have many children. And a husband, of course, not like Mother. He will play with the children, like their billy goat nudges his kids. Zel looks again at the goose, alone on a nest that will never be filled with goslings. "She makes me sad."

Mother stoops and picks a purple aster. She gently works it into Zel's right braid, so that it sits above her ear. She straightens Zel's smock. "Do you wish the goose wouldn't come back next year?" She swings her empty sack over her shoulder and walks on.

Zel stretches her arms out behind her, fingers spread like goose feathers in landing. She runs a few paces, then drops her arms. "No, I like her."

The path feels new. After all, they travel this path only

twice a year. Zel looks around. Berry bushes tangle the underbrush, but they are empty. The berries dried up weeks ago. Few fruits are more lovely than summer berries. Zel eyes the brush, her wish fervent and acute. But they wind their way downward, always through empty canes. She says softly, half to herself, "I'm hungry for raspberries."

"Look carefully." Mother's tone is light, much cooler than the midsummer air.

A tiny breeze stirs the leaves of an aspen. Its base is surrounded by prickly canes. Zel goes forward and gathers the berries. Just enough to fill both hands. "You knew they were here, didn't you?" She fills her mouth and walks beside Mother again. The berry juice runs down her chin. She wipes it away and licks her fingers. "How could you know these berries would be here, when all the other bushes are dry as dust?"

Mother opens her mouth as if to speak. But she says nothing. Her eyes are troubled.

A young hedgehog races from under a bush. At that moment the overhanging branch of a tree breaks and falls on it.

"No!" Zel runs and rolls the branch away. The little creature is stunned. It blinks at Zel, who coos as she checks its limbs. It scurries off. Zel returns to Mother's side. "I saw fear in its eyes. I wish I could have made it understand I meant no harm. I love animals, Mother. I want to talk to them."

"You practically do, Zel."

"In their language, I mean."

Mother smiles vaguely. She moves along more quickly and lightly now, taking Zel's hand. But Zel is too excited to walk. She drops Mother's hand and skips. She will be with people today all day long.

Zel loves seeing people. No one ever comes to visit their alm, but still Zel gets to see people often. So far this summer she has spied at least one of the herd boys every day. These are boys who live in the lower hills in winter. But in fair weather they take up residence with the mountain people in their scattered cabins. Once a week each boy takes a turn driving the communal herd across the alms for grazing. Zel has always wished that she and Mother had a cow to contribute to the herd so that the boys would stop by their alm. But Mother prefers goats. And whenever a herd boy crosses their grasses, Mother shoos him away before they can even exchange names.

But in town Mother can't shoo people away. Zel will get to see everyone, talk with everyone. Oh, town is wonderful.

The path through the woods comes out on the road. Far ahead two oxen pull a cart piled high with goods under an oilskin. On the road behind, Zel hears voices.

She glances at the family that walks beside a donkey loaded almost as high as the oxen cart. The market ahead will be full of donkeys like him, gossiping donkeys. "Hurry, Mother." Zel takes Mother's hand and pulls ahead.

Finally they pass through the covered bridge over the great river that empties into their lake, footsteps and voices resounding on the stone. When they emerge, the lake shines opaque green down to their left. It is long and flat this morning. Sometimes the lake moves from one end to the other like a thin good-weather quilt in a spring wind. There is a precipice near their home from which Zel can see almost the entire lake. When it moves in that special way, she wonders if the next lake over also moves. Perhaps today that lake is flat, too, inviting the foolish to walk on it.

The road winds along the side of the hill, passing below the opening of the grottoes. The son of the traveling handyman who patches their steep roof told Zel of those frigid hollows. The boy climbed through holes so narrow, he had to pull himself along on his stomach. He swam in black pools full of lime and vomited afterward. Zel listened and shivered. The boy gave her a cave rock, red from iron. But when Zel showed it to Mother, Mother snatched it and threw it from a cliff. Mother won't abide gifts. Zel painted caves dripping with purple-red mulberry stain for weeks after. When she looked at them, she shivered. And when she shivered, she remembered his question; he asked how she could bear living with no one but Mother way out on their alm. He said, "Don't you mountain people get lonely?"

Passing the grottoes, Zel drops Mother's hand and hugs herself with both arms to fend off the shivers.

At last, Zel and Mother arrive in town. They follow the cobblestones, winding through people and animals. The huge clock in the town tower seems to look down on the market square like an open eye. Zel and Mother stop at table after table—here piled high with paprika, bunches of parsley, savory, oregano; here covered with neat pyramids of cheese balls. The zesty smell of the Gruyère Mother buys tickles Zel's nose. They munch sweet rolls of white flour with raisins, citron, and cinnamon, glazed shiny with egg yolk.

Zel hums. She feels absorbed by the throng of people. She stops a moment, enjoying the sense of warmth and envelopment. But Mother nudges her along.

And here's the fruit stall they always visit. A girl Zel has talked with before hugs her warmly. A boy who looks to be the girl's brother sneaks strawberries into Zel's hand, the small, wild, exquisitely sweet kind. Mother grabs Zel by the wrist and the berries drop in the dust. How can Mother rush when it's been so long since they last came to town—six long, long months? Zel lags behind, forcing Mother to slow her pace.

Another vendor insists on slipping a licorice stick into Zel's pocket. Mother feigns ignorance of the act, perhaps because she knows Zel would protest if Mother refused this favorite of treats.

A third vendor, a woman Mother's age, leans forward. "The season's first grapes." She drops a small bunch of the green fruit in Zel's outstretched hands. Zel has them in her mouth before Mother can say no. But Mother doesn't seem to want to say no now. She presses through the crowds to the edge of the square.

Zel looks ahead. Her eyes alight on the mare that whinnies in protest as the blacksmith ties the fourth rope holding her in place. Merchants often leave their horses to be shod or to have their hooves filed while they sell their wares. Zel knows this because she and Mother have stood and watched the smith on past visits to town. "Mother, can we go watch?"

"I have errands to run. Stay here without me while I do them, will you?"

Zel's chest tightens. She has never been without Mother in town. Yet Zel has seen children walk unattended through the streets. Why, there, in front of the flower merchant, a child much smaller than Zel chooses foxgloves in blue and pink and white. And over there a girl of maybe fourteen or fifteen buys a slab of pork. Zel feels suddenly silly. "Of course, Mother. I'll be fine." And she will. This will be an adventure.

Mother touches Zel's cheek and a look of pure tenderness fills her eyes. She leaves.

Zel enters the smithy with a sense of anticipation that makes her almost giddy.

Chapter 2 ❖ ℳ o t h e r

I have been enjoying the unity of Mother and Daughter, weaving through the crowds like a single strand of yarn. As I leave Zel with the smith, I feel a sharp loss. I am sacrificing our wholeness, though the sacrifice is all for her sake. The only consolation is that the separation is temporary.

I am grateful to this unwitting smith and the beautiful virgin mare. They present the answer I sought: Now I can go off to buy the goods for Zel's birthday surprise. The flash of worry that crossed Zel's face when I suggested she stay alone at the smithy soothes my heart; my daughter will not stray. She is as bereft without me as I am without her.

I cut through the edge of the market. After thirteen

years of living on the alm, I am unused to the press and smell of human flesh. I feel foreign from the crowds, almost invisible.

I ease around a barrel of eels and find myself looking at the translucent eyes of newly dead fish. The fishmonger extols their virtues: The whitefish bring intelligence; the bream ensure healthy livers; the chub give vibrant skin. Our Aare River and Thuner Sea yield in abundance, and I am appropriately respectful.

The sound of wood slapping wood jerks me away. An old man has just been locked into the stocks behind me. A small crowd gathers. I listen. The man is called Wilhelm. His crime? Playing cards. The church police are foolish indeed, that they don't understand how evil comes in more subtle guises than card games. My neck prickles. It is as though a spider crawls slowly up my spine.

I walk quickly out of the square onto a narrow street. A wise dog sidles out of my path, glancing at me cautiously over his shoulder. I pass the public bathhouse and go up the second street on the left. Music wafts from the instrument maker's shop. He tests a new lute. I imagine its pearlike body, the belly pierced with holes in the pattern of a rose, the neck lined with brass frets. I gasp at its imagined beauty. My fingers itch to create—with needle and thread, with bow and fiddle. My mouth is dry with want. This lute captivates. A woman will buy it for her daughter who will give it to her daughter who will give it to her daughter. Just as my mother gave me my fiddle and as I will give the fiddle to Zel someday. The lute will have a history, as my fiddle does. Beauty will prevail.

I climb a flight of stairs and walk across flowered terraces that serve at once as footpaths in front of the second level of shops and as rooves of the shops below. I go directly to the house of the scribe.

"Ah, good day, madam." The scribe squints. Recognition flashes; his eyes glint with greed. "It's good to see you again."

I have every intention of satisfying his greed. There is no one else in the room, so I can look carefully before I choose.

The scribe moves immediately to a large stack of paper sheets. He holds his thumb and index finger apart the distance of a plum. "This much?"

Usually I buy a stack only the thickness of a grape. The scribe is trying to lure me into being extravagant, the absurd little man. Perhaps business is bad. But today he needn't work at tricking me. I respond to my own compulsion. "Twice that."

"Very good." The scribe takes even more than twice and sets it on the scale. He puckers his lips as if to whistle, then looks quickly at me. He writes down the price of the paper in silence. "And ink?"

I am already standing before the enormous jars. I close my eyes and will myself to see: The mare blows hot and soft on Zel's cheeks. The girl is happy and safe. I open my eyes. The scribe stands before me, holding a small empty bottle, ready to fill it. I point, not anticipating my own words, but content as they come out. "That, and that, and that."

The scribe's hands rush to the task. He is so excited at the sale of three bottles, when he expected the usual single one, that he almost spills.

I spy goose quills on the upper shelf. Normally Zel finds quills and sharpens them herself. But these are large, strong and supple, cut to fine points. I can already hear her delight. "And a quill. A tall one."

Everything fits snug in the bottom of my cloth bag, and there is still plenty of room. The scribe accompanies me to the door, half hunched over, an almost friendly curve to his mouth. Such crass people, whose warmth can be bought with a coin.

I come out of the scribe's hurriedly and am knocked hard. My cloth bag falls to the ground.

"Forgive me." The young man picks up the bag and hands it to me. He is dressed in expensive clothes—a noble, for sure. "Are you all right?"

I take the bag. I don't like his handsome face and tight trousers. And I've never liked nobility. The days of nobility are past. The peasant revolution made sure of that. Towns have elections now. And why am I thinking like this? First I thought about the church police. Now I think about civil governance. Town is seductive. Dangerous. I catch my breath and slow my heart. This youth's blow has not fazed me. I have nothing to do with these people. Zel is my only focus. I dismiss him with a nod.

"Good day." He races off.

I open the bag and check. The bottles of ink are intact. I close it and pick my way carefully, on the alert for rushing youths. But that one appears to have been alone.

The cloth merchant's shop is busy. A woman and two girls who look to be her daughters cut and fold material. I walk behind the customers, peering over shoulders.

I have decided to make Zel a new dress for her birthday, which comes in but four days. The girl's body is already changing, and the dress must be cut to accommodate the changes as they exaggerate themselves. The cloth must be of the right color, the right feel, the right swing when she twirls.

By the time it is my turn, I have made my selection. The sleeves will be emerald, like our lake in autumn; the bodice and skirt will be yellow cream, the color of the first saxifrage blooms; the apron will be emerald again, tying behind. The clerk makes approving remarks. I don't need her approval, yet I am glad she can see the value of my choices.

I spy cotton lace. I finger it gingerly.

"Perfect," murmurs the woman.

It will grace the bodice and skirt. Yes. I take extra to

make bows for Zel's golden braids. Next I pick out the threads. They are of many colors, but mainly emerald. Emerald is the color of life and hope. Zel is these things.

"Is this for your daughter?" The woman gives an ingratiating smile as she wraps my purchases in burlap.

I know she makes conversation only because she wants my future business. Yet I am glad she has guessed. I nod, knowing my pride shows.

"A young lady, no doubt? Turning twelve?"

Is the woman a mind reader? "Thirteen."

"Ah. So there's a man in the picture now? She'll be wed within the year, is that it?" The woman's voice is oil in water. "The stars favor weddings this year. You are wise."

I blanch. Zel will not be wed within the year. No. She must not leave me. This dress-to-be is perfect. Why has the clerk tainted my gift with her mundane talk of marriage? I am filled with elation at the thought of Zel's beauty in this dress and dread at the thought that anyone other than me should appreciate that beauty. The contradictory emotions merge hatefully, indiscretely, so that I cannot pick them apart.

I would hiss at the clerk, as I hissed at the crazy goose. I could whisper to her of berries that turn poisonous as they roll into her mouth, of greens that catch in her throat and choke. But I don't. She says no more. She will never know Zel. Her talk of marriage will never fall on Zel's ears.

I half glide from the shop, heady with the fineness of my purchase. I will go to the candy shop for the colored sugar balls with anise seed centers, the ones Zel loves. Then I can run to Zel and let her lead me through the rest of the marketplace. I will watch where her eyes light; I will indulge her small desires. Treats bring a glow to her cheeks. I will bask in that glow.

We will be together. Mother and Zel. Forever.

Chapter 3 ❖ *Zel*

el walks closer to the skittish horse. Its coat shines from recent brushing. Its legs are slender, unlike farm draft horses. It is framed by the four posts, with ropes attached to each post, as though begging for eyes to admire it. The white splotch on the horse's chest makes Zel think of stars.

The smith files a rear hoof, throwing his weight into each movement. The horse is large and could give him a kick he wouldn't forget for weeks.

She's a mare, but she seems as spirited as a stallion. There are two other horses waiting to be shod. Their chests are wide from pulling, their mouths thick from the bit. Zel can sense their docility. This mare is different.

Sweat drips into the smith's eyes, but he doesn't take the time to wipe his brow. He works quickly, anxiously. The mare makes nervous, rapid movements.

Zel is curious about the tension in the air. She moves like the mare, from foot to foot. The mare throws back her head. Zel tips back her head. The mare breathes heavily. Zel steps softly—close, so close that her own breath comes heavy on the mare's muzzle. The animal grows quiet. Zel places her hands on the mare's bony head; then she touches her own face, fingering the bones of her eye sockets. She thinks of how alike they are.

The smith finishes that hoof and walks to the water barrel to refresh himself before starting on the next. "Oh." He looks at Zel with surprise on his face. "Don't stand so close. You'll spook her." But his words lose their force even as he speaks, for it is obvious to anyone that his words are false.

Zel runs her hand again down the hard center of the horse's head to the spongy lips. The mare's lips open and close, and with a quick toss of the head she eats the aster Mother wove into Zel's braid. Zel laughs. She feels the smith's stare. She turns and smiles at him.

The smith dips a cup into the water barrel and splashes his face. "Have a way with animals, do you?"

Zel is pleased and embarrassed at the praise. "Do you have a carrot? Or an apple maybe? She'd really like one."

The smith laughs. "I'd be a poor man for sure if I fed every creature I tended to."

Zel thinks of the garden they have at home. There is no lack of carrots. And of the orchard. There is no lack of apples, even now in early July. Everything thrives under Mother's quick and knowing hands. Next time Zel comes to market, she'll have to bring some of both. It will be winter then, but carrots and apples will still be fragrant and sweet, wrapped in dry leaves and stored in the small cave they use as a cellar.

Zel gives a quiet nicker. She pulls the slice of brown bread from her pocket. The mare's nostrils quiver; she stamps a forefoot.

"She's restless this morning 'cause she's not used to me." The smith settles himself on a stool behind the mare. "My brother's the one as generally tends to her. But he got called away to a foaling."

Zel speaks a bit more firmly. "I think she'd like bread."

The smith grunts in reply. Then he sings to himself and goes back to work on the other hind hoof.

"Bread is for people," comes a new voice.

Zel jerks her head sharply to the right. A youth of maybe fifteen or sixteen has entered the stable. There is nothing decorative about his clothing. Still, the cloth of his shirt, though opaque and of an ordinary cream yellow, is so tightly woven it looks as though it were one piece, like the thinnest sliver of cedar bark. He hasn't the look of one who has ever skipped a meal. Yet his words suggest hunger. "Would you like some?" She holds the bread out toward him.

"You're offering me peasant bread?" The youth takes it without touching her fingers. He breathes deeply of its pungent aroma. He breaks off a corner, chews slowly. "You made this?"

"I helped Mother." Zel did some of the kneading, after all.

The youth takes another bite. "It's not bad." He looks Zel up and down.

Zel shifts uncomfortably under his gaze. The mare presses against her chest, asking to be petted again. Zel leans into the pressure of the mare's head, grateful for the excuse to give the horse her attention. She scratches the honey-colored coat with vigor, her hands moving upward.

The mare throws her head with a loud snort.

"Be careful," says the youth. "Meta's left ear hurts."

Zel drops her hands. Meta. A fine and proper name.

"The hind hooves are finished," says the smith, his

voice gruff. He comes around the horse and sees the youth. He clears his throat. "The forehooves can wait, sire." He leans the large file against the water barrel.

"Take a look in this ear."

"It might be best to wait for my brother."

The youth shakes his head. "I came back now just to tell you about her ear." He glances at Zel, then back to the smith. His voice grows strained. "Take a look."

Zel watches this exchange in wonder. The youth owns the horse named Meta. So he is definitely a youth of means. But the smith is old enough to be his father. Zel has seen young and old interact. She knows that youth shows deference to age. Who is this youth who orders the smith around?

"As you wish, sire." The smith rubs his hands on a cloth. He pulls a short rope and a wooden peg from his pocket. The rope is much finer than those that hold the mare to the posts. He threads the rope through a hole in one end of the peg and ties it into a loop. Then he grabs the mare's top lip and slips the loop around it. He turns the peg, tightening the loop. The mare's lip bunches together and protrudes over her now bared teeth.

Zel understands immediately: This way the smith can look in the mare's left ear, knowing pain will stop her from moving her head even the slightest bit.

Still, the horse is clever. She stomps with her left forefoot. She will not yield gently.

The smith hesitates. And Zel can see the problem: How will he be able to work on the mare if he must use one hand to hold the peg? His Adam's apple moves up and down as he swallows. "This is my brother's type of task. Your horse knows my brother's hands. Tomorrow would be a better day."

The youth lifts his chin. Zel can see the muscles of his cheeks tighten.

She speaks on impulse: "I'll hold her head still. It's the lip rope that she despises." Zel deftly takes the peg and untwists it before they can object. The loop slips off. The mare lowers her head and presses against Zel once more. Zel hugs both arms around the mare's jaw and rests her cheek on the flat between the mare's eyes. She wills herself to radiate quiet. The mare stands perfectly still.

"Go ahead," says the youth.

The smith looks in the horse's left ear. He pokes with one finger. His face goes blank. Then he looks relieved. He jams thumb and index finger into the ear and yanks. He holds the tick up, its legs wiggling in the air, so fat with blood that its hard outer shell shines as if it would explode. "Nothing but a tick, sire." The smith exhales loudly. He walks to the forge and throws the tick into the coals. In an instant it is black. It pops.

"Good work," says the youth.

The smith seems encouraged now, almost eager. "I suppose I could do the forehooves if you like, sire."

The youth doesn't look at the smith or the mare. His eyes are on Zel. "Yes."

The smith goes to work.

Zel combs the mare's forelock with her fingers. Ticks are hideous creatures. She's glad to be rid of it. Yet its bursting unsettled her. She can hear Mother's refrain in her head: She must toughen up, be sensible. But she's all ajangle. The youth's eyes unsettle her as well. She clutches the halter as though the mare has threatened to run off, but the mare has done nothing. It is Zel who has the urge to run off.

The youth is practically staring at Zel now. He blurts out, "I owe you something." His hand goes to the coin pouch at his waist.

"What?" Zel brushes off her hands in amazement and steps back from the mare, who immediately stomps. The smith grunts. Zel laughs and steps forward again. She strokes Meta's neck and looks at the youth. At his eyes. And she knows: Even in such giving words he is imperious. He treats her as he treats the smith. But she didn't render a service for him; she did it for the mare's sake. And she certainly didn't do it for money. "You owe me nothing."

"You give me bread, you enchant my horse, and you want nothing in return." The youth rubs the back of his neck.

Zel likes his face. Almost against her will. His fine

brow furrows and a muscle in his jaw twitches. Yes, Zel likes the face of this spoiled youth very much.

"There must be something you want." He drops his hand and looks at her intently.

His eyes pry. Zel shifts again in her increasing discomfort.

A small smile plays at the corners of the youth's mouth. "Something."

Heat rises in Zel's cheeks. She needs to feel the cool wind of the alm in her face. She shakes her head.

His eyes twinkle. "Think hard." His voice teases. As though he takes pleasure in her discomfort. Or worse—as though he knows her heart's desires when she doesn't know them herself.

Or does she? "Yes," says Zel all of a sudden. She nods quickly. The idea is perfect. "Yes."

The youth looks satisfied. "Name your price."

Zel can hardly keep from shouting. "A goose egg."

The youth comes a step forward. He cocks his head in disbelief. "A goose egg?"

"A fertilized one that is still warm from the goose." She can carry it home inside her bodice. She can breathe hot on it. Then she can slide it under the goose. Won't the lonely goose be overjoyed when the shell cracks and the gosling peeps? "It will make a goose I know very happy."

The youth grins. "A warm goose egg. All right. I'll be back shortly." The youth leaves, almost at a run.

Zel watches him go. His calf muscles bulge. He must be a good climber, like Zel. She never tires of wandering.

The smith finishes the last hoof. He straightens up and rotates his shoulders. He looks at Zel circumspectly. "You don't live in town, do you?"

"No."

"Too bad." He leans against a post. "Do you take care of your own donkey? Your own oxen?"

"We don't have oxen or donkeys. We have goats. And chickens." She doesn't mention the rabbits. Everyone has rabbits.

The smith nods. "Tell you what. Whenever you're in town, stop by. If I can use your help, I'll pay you." He jerks his chin toward Zel's worn smock. "You could use the money, eh?"

It seems everyone wants to pay Zel today. Town is a place of give and take. But Mother has enough money for their town needs. And what would Zel do with money on the alm? "I'll come again in winter. If I can be of use, that will be payment enough."

Mother arrives, her sack full. She looks sharply at the smith. "Come now, Zel. We mustn't be a bother."

The smith shakes his head. "No bother." He looks as if

he would say more, but Mother's eye is unmistakable: His words are unwelcome.

Zel is annoyed at Mother's protectiveness. Her first venture alone in town was fabulous. "I have to wait." She chooses her words for the most effect: "Someone is coming with a gift for me."

"A gift?" Mother speaks slowly. Her tone shows her displeasure. "What kind of gift?"

"A goose egg." Zel laughs at her own words. She hopes Mother's irritation will melt away, just as her own has. "A fertilized one."

Mother nods. "A gift for the goose, then, not really for you."

"You don't have to wait." The smith looks at Mother nervously. And now the mare turns a yellow, wary eye. The smith says, "When the egg comes, I'll save it for you. You can stop by and get it on your way home this afternoon."

"But it must stay warm." Zel clasps her hands together.

The smith looks at Zel's face. His own softens a bit. "Warm as a mother goose's bottom, eh?" He points at her with a finger callous from work. "I'll keep it safe."

Zel has no choice but to trust him. "Thank you."

Mother offers a hand to Zel. She smiles. "I guess this is a day for gifts."

The smith raises a brow.

"It's my birthday on the sixth," says Zel, suddenly thrilled at the thought. But, in fact, giving the egg to the goose will be more wonderful than getting the papers and ink Zel knows are in Mother's sack.

"Let's go find the farmer who sells that lettuce you love so much." Mother wiggles the fingers of the extended hand.

"Oh, yes." Zel has a taste for a lettuce with small, round leaves that a traveling peddler once gave her. After that, whenever they came to the market, she sought it out and always from the same farmer, who calls her by name. She has asked Mother to grow this lettuce, but Mother refuses, without explanation. Zel can't wait to make a salad of it tonight.

Maybe today she'll ask the farmer for seeds so that next spring she can grow it herself. It's time she tended a garden. After all, in not too many years she'll be making salad for her own children.

And she must find that oxen cart that was covered with the oilskin and gaze upon its now revealed treasures. And she must listen for the melon crier. And she must drink from the well at the edge of the marketplace as she always does while Mother leans against the huge iron rock beside it. And she must gawk at the flower-bedecked central fountain. And she must visit the cheese-maker to see the giant copper pot where the milk scalds. And, oh, there's so much to do.

Zel brushes Mother's hand without taking it as she leaves the smithy. She reaches into her pocket and draws out the licorice stick. She puts it in the side of her mouth and chews. The taste of market day enthralls her.

Chapter 4 ❖ Konrad

hot goose egg. Konrad finds himself running. His feet are happy. He has met a remarkable girl, the friend of a goose, an enchantress of horses, who bakes bread heavy with molasses and looks at him with eyes dark and glowing.

As Konrad passes the printer's shop, the smell of leather and parchment makes him laugh for no reason. He shouts a greeting to the barber surgeon who extracted his father's brown tooth and replaced it with an ivory one last fall. The man waves in a rush, his hand aglitter with rings.

Konrad spins around and knocks into a woman coming out of the house of the scribe. Her bag falls to the ground. He picks it up, apologizes, races off. Faster, past all the bustling crowds. The whole world seems to rush, caught in errands, but none so wondrous as Konrad's.

Konrad arrives at the castle stables and there's Franz, rubbing oil into a saddle. "Franz!"

Franz blinks into the sunlight. "Yes, sire?"

Konrad imagines himself placing the egg in the girl's hands and the gratitude on her face. He can do it quickly, a little thing, a gallant gesture. "I need a goose egg."

Franz blinks again. "You're hungry? The midday meal will be within the hour."

"It's not for ..." Konrad stops. He realizes he doesn't want to explain to Franz that he's on an errand for a mere country girl. "I need a goose egg." He circles Franz, then stops by the saddle and drums his fingers.

Franz moves his chin in and out. He reminds Konrad of a turtle. "We don't keep geese."

"I know that." Of course Konrad knows that.

"But we've got chickens. I can get you a big chicken egg if that'll do."

"That won't do at all." The girl would never accept a chicken egg. Konrad's hands are now combing through his hair. He spins and looks out over the town toward the lake. "Maybe there's a wild goose nest hereabouts?"

"Wild geese have already hatched their broods."

Of course that's so. The edge of the lake has had clusters of goslings for weeks now. Even Konrad, immersed in his lessons, has noticed that. The girl has tricked Konrad. She asked for a deceptively simple gift—and he arrogantly assured her he'd get it—but it's impossible to find. Does she take him for a fool?

"Annette could cook you up a dozen eggs." Franz pats Konrad's arm. "Go in the kitchen, sire."

Konrad remembers the girl's boldness as she held Meta's head still. Her long fingers were sure and quick and graceful. Her hair was pulled so tightly into those braids that there was a white line down the center of the back of her head. He imagines the girl with her hair loose.

He has to get that egg.

Annette, who knows about most practical matters, must know about geese. Konrad used to tag after her when he was little, and she'd show him so many wonders. Konrad runs for the kitchen.

"Ah, and it's a second good morning to you, young sire." Annette bastes a pig over the fire. Fat drips from the spit with a hiss.

"What's the occasion?"

"The count returns tonight. Earlier than expected." Annette tucks a wisp of her hair behind her ear. She wipes her hands on a towel and pours him a mug of ale.

Konrad takes the mug and gulps. "Annette, I need a goose egg." He holds up a hand to ward off questions. "It's urgent."

"A goose egg." Annette purses her lips.

Konrad puts down the mug and paces. He is used to solving problems quickly—and much more challenging problems than finding a goose egg. He slaps the fist of his right hand into his left palm over and over.

But Annette is not to be rushed. "Have a bite to eat while I give this some thought." She takes a strudel down from the high board and sets it on the table.

Konrad has no time for eating.

As though Annette can read his mind, she says, "Eat. It's the kind you like best."

Konrad rips himself a hunk, rich with prunes and nuts. It chews more easily than the girl's bread; it is sweeter and finer. Yet, given the choice, he'd take the girl's black bread anytime. The girl. Why, oh, why is all this taking so long?

Annette nods slowly. "There's a farmer who raises geese just out of town, lakeside."

Konrad grabs her hands. "Which road do I take?"

She steps back in confusion, but her hands are caught in his. "It's faster to run the path behind the church."

Konrad kisses Annette's cheek. "You're wonderful."

She gives a small, hesitant smile. "He raises swans, too." She turns for a peck on the other cheek.

"Who gives a fig for swans?" But Konrad kisses Annette's other cheek anyway.

He descends the covered staircase at a run. He passes

the church's octagonal tower and barges his way through the crowds.

He arrives at the path still running, though the loose rocks tumble away under his feet. The path narrows. Konrad has to use more care. He should have asked how far it would be. Sweat makes his shirt stick between his shoulders. He wipes at the back of his neck and runs. Too much time is passing. How long will the girl stay at the smithy? Why was she there in the first place? And where's the cursèd goose farm?

The path skirts downhill through high grasses. It turns, and Konrad comes upon the farm at the same moment that he hears the honking. Yes, there's the goose yard, and the swans are mixed right in with them. Everything lies open before him. There's not even a fence to climb over. Beside a small outbuilding is a giant nest. Konrad approaches, and the honks get louder. Two cobs come as one, on the attack, wings spread, necks out front full length, huge bills open.

Konrad pivots on his heel and runs flat out. But the swans are upon him, beating with their wings, pecking at his ankles. "Help!" He falls, slams his chin in the dirt, birds on his back, honks louder than hell's fury.

The birds are suddenly off him, honking still, walking stupidly into each other.

"Serves you right, thief," says a small boy. He stands over Konrad, a long stick in his hand.

"Thief?" Konrad rubs at his ankles, at his back. "Who are you calling a thief?"

A cob approaches again. The boy whacks warningly at the bird. It trumpets. "Hush!" He turns to Konrad. "You wanted to take a bird, didn't you?"

"Only an egg. A goose egg."

The boy swings his stick. The cobs finally lose interest and wander off. "Can't you tell swans from geese?"

"Of course I can. I wasn't looking at the birds." Konrad points. "I was looking at that nest."

"That's a swan's nest." There's a poorly concealed edge of disgust in the boy's voice.

Konrad stands up. "Get me a goose egg. Now."

The boy puts his stick under his arm and holds out his hand. "Money first."

"I'm Count Konrad."

The boy eyes the simple cut of Konrad's clothes dubiously. Then he seems to decide they're fine enough. He nods. "It'll cost you double, then."

Konrad snorts. It's not the money; it's the boy's attitude that irritates him. "Who owns this farm?"

"Doesn't matter who owns it. We work it." The boy still holds his hand outstretched.

Konrad squares his shoulders. There is a disturbing element of truth in the boy's words. "The egg's got to be fertilized."

The boy nods.

Konrad drops a coin in the boy's hand.

The boy turns and runs.

"Hey, wait." Konrad runs after him.

The boy goes around the outbuilding, Konrad at his heels. He stops at a nest and lifts an egg with one hand, swinging his stick with the other. The geese attack immediately. He shoves the egg at Konrad. "Hold it."

Konrad cradles the egg in both hands. He stays close behind as the boy smacks at the geese with his stick.

"Now take your egg and go," says the boy in a half shout. He runs off toward the farmhouse.

Konrad races for the path. The geese race after. He wraps both arms around the egg now. He is scrabbling up the rocky path and the honks are falling behind him, further and further. He finally stops for breath.

Konrad looks at the egg. What if it's a dud? There's no way to tell from just looking. He smells it. It smells of grass and farmy dung. He holds it to his ear. Silent. But there is a heat and denseness about its silence. The gosling lives.

Konrad wipes the sweat from his brow. He holds the egg before him and goes up the long path to the rear of the church. He takes the covered staircase down into town, slipping easily through the market crowds now, as though the mission of the egg has bestowed a new agility.

The smith is shoeing a gelding.

Konrad walks up behind him. "Where is she?"

The smith straightens up. "In that stall right there. No problem at all."

Konrad looks in the stall. Meta looks back at him. "But where's the girl?"

"Oh, she left with her mother long ago."

"She didn't wait for her egg?"

The smith looks at the egg. "They'll come for it."

Konrad clutches the egg to his chest. "When?"

"After they've finished their marketing, I suppose."

Anger rushes at Konrad with the sudden fierceness of the farm birds. "I can't be expected to wait. I have important tasks. And I went through a lot of trouble to get this egg."

The smith knits his brows. He reaches for the egg with anxious hands. "Of course not, sire. You're to leave it with me. I'll give it to them."

Konrad twists his body away from the smith's hands. No peasant girl can treat him this way: ask for an egg, then run off before he brings it back. The girl is impudent. Maddening. Konrad stands speechless in his wrath.

The smith lowers his head a bit. "The egg, sire. I'll make sure she gets it."

Konrad doesn't want to part with the egg. Not this way. He has imagined the response of the girl as she receives the egg. He has seen her face light up before—he expected to see it light up again. And now he is to be cheated of that response and in such a humiliating way.

The smith gestures to a small pile of straw not far from the furnace. "That's where I'll set it. The lass and I agreed." His voice coaxes. "Give it here, sire."

Konrad walks to the straw and puts the egg down. A sudden urge to snatch it back seizes him. He clasps his hands together and tries to look calm. It would never do for anyone to know that a peasant girl, a simple child with braids, could upset him. He thinks of her high brow; her thin, long nose; her questioning eyes; and then tries to shake her image from his head.

Konrad puts the blanket and saddle on Meta. He slaps his hat on his head and rides out, down to the main road. It's past time for the midday meal, but Konrad is too impatient to sit at the table. He'll go directly to his afternoon task. Today he is to inspect crops. One-tenth of those crops belong to him, as landlord. He must approximate their yield, so the farmer can't cheat. Then he will go for a country ride. This is his mare. An early birthday present from his father, the count, who went to Baden for a meeting of the legislature. Annette said Father returns tonight. Konrad will greet him along this very road, astride Meta. He sits tall now. If he held a lance, he would look like one of the soldiers of Christ in the beloved red-and-blue stained-glass window of the church directly across from his bedroom balcony.

After more than an hour, Konrad cuts off the main road and follows a country track that twists and turns with the rising curves of the foothills. A quiet heat hovers above the neat rows of cultivation. Summer is lush.

Yes, Konrad will definitely take a long ride later. He can stop at an inn for a drink and a light meal. And he will forget the goose-egg girl. With her country shoes and country smock. He will forget the braids, the eyes.

He rides up to the farmhouse at last.

But he doesn't dismount. All he can think of is the eyes. Blackest of eyes. Eyes that follow him.

When Konrad looked at the girl this morning, she seemed unaware that he watched; yet she couldn't be. She's old enough to know the attentions of men. She must have some country boy who gawks at her. A bumbling boy who chews grass.

Konrad's jaw tenses at the thought. His throat thickens. He turns around and rides back to the smithy, urging Meta faster and faster.

The smith's face drops at the sight of Konrad. His eyes dart to Meta's legs. "Ah, sire. Will you be needing something?"

"Did the girl collect her egg?"

Relief eases the smith's face. "With much happiness."

Of course. How stupid of him not to have found an excuse to wait for her. He swings his leg over Meta's neck and jumps to the ground. "Is she coming back today?"

"No, sire." The smith waits. His eyes seem to appraise Konrad. "There's something you need, sire?"

Konrad gives a little snort. The girl owes him a thank you. "The girl, what's her name?"

The smith sticks his finger in his ear, as though the act will improve his memory. He looks like a dolt. Konrad would like to see him attacked by a goose. "Ah, yes." The smith points his dirty finger at Konrad. "Zel. That's what her mother called her."

"That's an odd name. Where does this Zel live?"

"Don't know, sire."

Konrad sees a hint of mirth in the smith's eyes. What insolence. He climbs up on Meta. "Find out." He leaves.

Frustration gnaws. Konrad can inspect the crops tomorrow, before his classics tutor comes. For now, he needs distraction—song and dance. But the new church has banned secular music. Damn.

His mind goes to Zel's braids. Why is he thinking of that wretched girl's braids?

He rides Meta around to the castle stables. In an instant he knows Father is back, for there is Franz rubbing down Father's horse.

Konrad slides off the horse. He bursts into the kitchen and races through to the Knights' Hall. "Father!" The heavy tapestries on the walls absorb his shout. "Father!"

Father and son embrace. They kiss one another on alternating cheeks, three times. Then the men who have gathered at Father's return, the men of the small council that governs their city-state, greet Konrad with kisses.

"I have another birthday surprise for you." The count beams.

Konrad smiles. Another present is exactly what he needs to salvage this day from a rotten ending.

The count turns to the men. "An announcement."

Konrad's chest swells in delighted anticipation.

The count smiles benevolently at Konrad. "Konrad is betrothed."

Konrad stands stock-still and stares at Father.

The count laughs. "Dumbfounded with joy, are you? Let me tell you about the young lady."

No. Konrad won't hear about this unknown girl. Not today. Definitely not today.

"Ah, she's a beauty, she is," the count is saying.

In an instant this has become the most terrible day of Konrad's life.

REJECTION

Chapter 5 ❖ ꝣ e l

el carries the goose egg inside her smock. Mother is ahead on the trail. The lettuce Zel loves peeks out of the top of Mother's sack. Zel knows there are gifts within the sack. She smiles. Her birthday is the most luscious event of the year.

Every few minutes Mother bends to pick up a snail. Mother has already filled both Zel's pockets with the flaring yellowish mushrooms that abound in the damp woods, among the marsh marigolds. They taste fine, oh, so fine, fried in butter with salt. Now Mother works on filling her own pockets with snails.

Zel will cook these mushrooms and snails herself and surprise Mother. The youth at the smithy asked if she'd made the bread she offered him. She wished she could have said yes, rather than admitting she'd only helped.

Zel is not hungry right now, though. Before they left the market, she and Mother bought onion cakes, steaming from the oven, tender and savory. Mother has promised they will have onion soup on Zel's birthday. Few foods cannot be improved with the onions that grow in un-abashed exuberance in this land.

When they get to the wooden bridge, Zel sees that the goose is not on her nest on the other side. She revels in her luck. It is yet daylight, though it is nearly ten o'clock. The goose must be off feeding before she settles down to sleep. They would have been home more than an hour ago if they had traveled at their normal pace. But Zel insisted on walking slowly for the sake of the egg. Zel moves carefully, carefully over the bridge and places the egg gently, gently in the nest. She is certain that the bird can count at least to five. She selects the largest rock, the one closest to the size of the egg, and steals it from the nest, so that the number the goose sits on will be constant. She looks around. The ground is scattered with goose feathers. She takes a few and rubs them on the true egg. Perhaps they will cover the scent of her humanity.

Mother nods in approval. "Come, Zel. Bedtime."

Zel and Mother enter the cottage. Mother's kiss is sweet and cool. She unravels Zel's braids and combs her hair till it's smooth as water. Zel yields herself to the small bed.

Mother sprinkles lavender on the foot of Zel's bed; then she plays the fiddle. Every night of her life Zel has gone to bed on the sound of Mother's fiddle.

When Mother is convinced Zel sleeps, she leaves to do chores. Her rapid footsteps cover the kitchen.

Zel lies with her eyes closed. Her fingers reach under the edge of the bedroll and touch the paper that holds the lettuce seeds she convinced the vendor to give her today while Mother was bargaining with a passing traveler for an exotic fruit.

Zel tosses and turns. She can't get comfortable. What would it be like to be balled up inside a shell? Can the gosling hear the world outside? Zel listens.

Finches, starlings, chickadees, cuckoos. The birds chirp loudly. Birds and waterfalls, those are the sounds of summer. In winter the rage of storm winds and the deafening crack of ice alternate with total quiet. But summer is always noisy. Zel lies in the coverlet of summer noise. Her ears ring with the cowbells she heard on the way to market. And now she hears the pop of the tick at the smithy. It turns her stomach. She hears the almost deep voice of the youth. Something within her lurches.

She sees him chewing the bread. Rubbing his neck. Shifting his head from side to side. Her skin comes alive as she thinks of him. Her fingers lace together as though combing the mare's mane. The star on the chest of the mare twinkles in the skies of her dreams.

Chapter 6 ❧ *Mother*

I wake early. It is barely dawn.

I make a bread dough, kneading extra long so that the texture will be extra fine. I set it to rise. When next I punch it down, I will work in raisins. I think of the small noises of enjoyment Zel made yesterday eating the sweet buns at the market. I will add nuts as well. The chores of the morning satisfy more than usual today.

I go outside and milk the first nanny I catch. Only a small bucketful today. But no matter. Zel and I are still overfull from market day. I uproot a lone edelweiss, taking care to keep the dirt packed around its roots.

When I come back inside, I place the edelweiss in a cup on the table. I give a twist to the press on the new cheese I am making. Then I pick the snails from the meal I set them in last night. They have gorged themselves. I dump the bucket, slapping the bottom hard, then put the snails back in. In a day or two they will pass the meal, and their digestive tracts will be empty of all impurities. They will be ready to eat. I can steam them and serve them with chives. I can fry the mushrooms that make Zel smile.

I check: Zel sleeps still. This is a moment for private work. I will finish the ordinary chores later.

I shut myself in the kitchen. I can't remember when the door to the kitchen was last closed in summer. In winter we often sleep in the kitchen with a fire going, our bedrolls on the floor. But in summer that door stands open.

I spread the materials on the table and smooth them with hands that flutter, I am so excited. Zel has never had a real dress. She has worn children's smocks all her life. Zel will be stunning in this dress. And it won't be the traditional dirndl of the land of my childhood. It will be unique, more beautiful a garment than even I have ever made before, though its beauty will never rival the beauty of Zel. Still, it will be befitting of her.

I sew the skirt first. I am fast at stitching. The kitchen is only just reasonably sunlit by the time I finish. I fold the skirt carefully and set it aside. Now I cut the sleeves. I cut with precision, for the sleeves will be fitted from wrist to elbow, then loose to the shoulder. The click of needle on thimble goes faster and faster.

I check on Zel; the girl sleeps.

I add lace to the cuffs. Nothing gaudy, just enough to show the refinement of Zel's spirit. I cut the bodice. It will have many darts. I stand at the table and plan. I will embroider the bodice in a pattern of wings, for Zel moves so gracefully, it is almost as though she flies.

"Mother?"

"Ah, you're up. Get dressed. Then I'll open the door." I fold the three pieces of the bodice. I wrap all in burlap and store it on the shelf. I open the door.

Zel falls into the room. She laughs in embarrassment at having been caught listening at the door. "Something for my birthday, my birthday, my birthday." She dances. Her eyes settle instantly on the bundle on the shelf. "What is it?"

I smile. "Would you like gruel?"

Zel laughs. "Shall I guess?"

I fill our bowls from the jar of dried grains and nuts and fruits. It is a breakfast full of energy. I keep this child strong.

Zel sits on her chair and picks up her spoon. "Papers and inks," she says gaily.

I am happy she guesses only part. Secrets are delicious, like plum pudding in water. "If you promise not to guess anymore, I'll give you your first gift now. But your second must wait till your real birthday."

"I promise."

I go to the cloth bag and put the stack of paper on the table. Then slowly, dramatically, I place the bottles of ink beside the paper: one, two, three.

Zel gasps. She holds the bottles up to the sunlight.

"They are glorious, Mother. Oh, thank you." She takes a piece of paper off the stack and smooths it onto the table. "I'll draw that little donkey. The one with the tall load."

I am completely happy. "Finish your breakfast first."

Zel eats quickly. Then she dips her quill into the black ink. I watch her deft movements, her eyes intent on the fine lines, lines so much finer than she can make with the charcoal she usually uses for drawing. I know the girl chose to draw the donkey in order to begin with the black ink. The indigo and crimson, the more precious colors, will be savored later. I understand the method.

I relax now into my own kind of enjoyment. I close my eyes and see a sparrow hawk swoop for the sheer fun of flight, right over our rooftop. Then I allow my vision to wander across our alm, taking pleasure in the curve of each leaf, the hue of each petal.

"No!" I drop my spoon in my bowl and jump to my feet.

"What, Mother? What is it?"

I race from the room, from the cottage, Zel behind me. I run straight toward the goose nest but halt before I reach it. "You stupid bird." The words burst from my mouth in small explosions of air.

Zel picks up the egg the goose has rolled from the nest. She holds it in front of her as though it's an offering of sorts. She looks at the goose, who fixes the two of us with one eye. "Please, goose," Zel whispers.

"Please. This can be your child." She licks her lips in concentration.

"Do it, Zel." Need almost snaps my voice. The bird must take back the egg. For Zel's sake. "Make her accept it."

Zel takes a step toward the goose. The goose leans her neck toward Zel. Zel takes another step, still holding the egg in outstretched hands. The goose doesn't move. A third step. The goose flexes her wings. Zel sinks to the ground. She walks on her knees toward the goose.

I stare. My daughter moves like a supplicant before the host. Where did she learn such behavior? I have never taken Zel to any church. I cannot enter churches.

The goose spreads her wings more, though she remains on folded legs. Zel bends over so her elbows touch the ground. She crawls.

Now my daughter seems the penitent. I recall scenes from my childhood. I stood in the crowds and watched penitents on hands and knees, throwing ashes backward over their heads, calling for mercy and forgiveness. As if there really were mercy and forgiveness in this world. Will the goose yield? Is her heart as much rock as the eggs she gathers to her nest each summer?

She must yield. She must not be so merciless. Zel needs to see that the goose can love this foreign egg, this borrowed egg, with as much fervor—no, with more fervor—than its own mother. Zel needs that.

I need that.

I can barely breathe. Zel's hands move closer and closer to the nest edge. The bird must not attack Zel. If it does, Zel could drop the egg.

A morning glory vine creeps up the slope by the stream. It has almost reached the level of the bridge. I concentrate on that vine. The vine, energized and strong, twists and lengthens and curls itself across the ground and into the goose nest from behind, where neither Zel nor I can see it. It twines around the goose's feet, her folded legs. It holds the bird fast. I stumble back a step from the effort of growing the vine.

The goose spreads her wings full width. She opens her mouth, and her blue-gray tongue stands isolated, trilling the loud hiss. But she cannot rise.

Zel sets the egg on the inner curve of the nest. It rolls over once and rests against the goose's exposed side. Then Zel crawls backward and finally stands. She and I turn and walk toward the cottage.

I close my eyes. The goose gives up struggling. The morning glory shrinks away to the slope from which it came. I open my eyes.

Chapter 7 ❖ Zel

el stands at the window and watches the goose rearrange the sticks of her nest. She is as wordless as the egg. Zel knows much about birds. She has spent whole days watching them. Birds accept each other's eggs all the time. And geese, they love anything round. Zel cannot comprehend the goose's behavior.

But it is not the goose that matters. All Zel can think of now is the egg, this blameless egg that would have been a hatchling soon if Zel had not asked the youth to bring it to her, this egg that Zel may have doomed in her stupidity. Mother gives Zel too much credit. She told Zel to make the goose accept the egg. But Zel doesn't know how to coax this goose. Still, the goose allowed Zel to return the egg to the nest. There is room for hope. *Please, goose,* Zel begs in her head, *know this egg. For all that is good and beautiful and true, please.*

The goose rocks herself, settling deeper into the nest. Zel is encouraged. If only she could speak to the goose with her mind. *Goose,* she says in her head in easy rhythm, *goose goose goose.* The goose stretches her neck out to the heat of the sun. She seems to sleep.

Zel turns and goes back to the table. The urge to draw seizes her more ferociously than before. She bends over her work. A skinny donkey dances in the center of the paper. He has knobby, hairless knees, as though he knelt often. She draws a second donkey extending his muzzle to gladioli in a market stall.

Now she draws a boy who selects a flower for the donkey, his head cocked, his eyes teasing. Zel remembers the youth of yesterday, the clean curve to his jaw. And he had a dimple on only one cheek. His left.

Mother goes outside, carrying the egg basket. Zel lifts her head to watch her go. Normally the chore of gathering eggs falls on Zel. But Mother does it now. Zel knows Mother will also feed the rabbits. Whenever Zel is sad, Mother bustles about in this way. Mother does these chores now as a comfort to Zel, for she knows the fear Zel feels for the gosling.

Mother fears, too. Zel heard it in her voice. Zel leans over the cup with the edelweiss and gently brushes her cheek against the delicate petals. Then she walks over to the bowl of rising dough. She punches it down. There is a daring in her action: Normally she would ask Mother before interfering in something Mother had begun. Raisins form a pile beside the dough. Zel's hands are reckless today. She works the raisins in. Then she uses all her weight to force a twist to the press on the cheese Mother is making. There: Zel now comforts Mother as much as Mother comforts Zel.

Zel returns to the table and takes up her drawing

again. She hears Mother enter and set the eggs in a bowl. Her cheeks are taut with anticipation. What will Mother say when she realizes Zel has worked the raisins into the dough? Will she notice that the cheese press is tighter? Zel hears Mother take down the burlap-wrapped package from the shelf and go outside. That's all right. Mother will notice later.

Zel draws until the paper is full, well past midday.

"Mother." Zel stands respectfully in the kitchen and does not look out the window. She knows Mother sits outside working on a secret. "I'm ready for lunch. Won't you come in?"

Mother comes inside and puts the burlap-wrapped bundle on the shelf.

"Let me help," Zel is saying before Mother even has a chance to talk about what they will eat. Zel washes two kinds of lettuce—the small-leafed lettuce that is special to her and their own garden lettuce. She separates the leaves into two bowls. "My mouth waters already."

Mother laughs. "Your inherited love of that lettuce grows stronger every year." She slices a carrot.

Inherited? Zel's heart speeds up. "You never eat it."

"I like what we grow." Mother now shells peas. "Raw peas make a salad into a meal."

Zel moves very close to Mother. She makes the plea she has made many times. "Tell me about my father."

"I know nothing of him."

Zel is accustomed to Mother's answer, but this time she can prove her wrong. "He loves this lettuce; that much you know."

Mother opens her mouth, then quickly shuts it.

"Is that why you named me after the lettuce?"

Mother peels an onion. "You are clever, Zel." She hands Zel a tomato.

Zel slices, wishing she were clever enough to find a way to lure Mother into a real conversation about Father. Father. A name without an image. Zel doesn't even know if she ever saw her own father. "Do you want to see what I drew?"

"I was hoping you'd offer."

Zel wipes her hands on her smock and holds the paper up by the top corners before Mother's eyes.

"Who is the child?"

"No one, really. Do you like the donkeys?"

Mother sets the two salad bowls before the two chairs. She brings the dark loaf to the table and sits. Her face is quiet. Her voice comes out level and cold. "Do you know that boy?"

Zel shakes the paper insistently. "Don't you care about the donkeys? Look at them."

Mother looks dutifully at the drawing. "The donkeys don't act like donkeys."

Zel drops the paper on the table and puts her hands on her hips. "We don't own donkeys, so how do we know?

Maybe when donkeys are all alone, they dance and sing."
The idea is so absurd that Zel can't stay mad at Mother.
She laughs.

The edges of Mother's mouth twitch. "They aren't
alone."

"No, I guess they're not." Zel sits and munches salad.
The slight bite of the green juice excites her tongue. For
supper she can soft-boil two eggs and eat them with this
lettuce. She thinks of the folded paper hidden under her
bedroll that holds the lettuce seeds. Zel hasn't told
Mother about the spring garden she will have. Her own
garden.

These are her seeds. Her secret.

Chapter 8 ❧ *M o t h e r*

 have no appetite. The child Zel has drawn is
more handsome by far than the handyman's
son. Who is he?

Zel looks at me and speaks slowly. "The child does
look a little like a youth I met yesterday."

Her words come as if in response to my unspoken
question. Did my question enter her head? I didn't will it

to. I would be alarmed at this new possibility, but there is something more tangible to be alarmed at: "You met a youth." How old is this youth? Is he married? Has he set his eyes on Zel? Time grows swiftly short. Panic teases my skin. My arm hairs stand on end. "Was it he who gave you the goose egg?"

"How did you guess?" A look of pleasure spreads across Zel's face. She leans forward, as though revealing a puzzle that I can help her decipher. She begins timidly. "I did nothing for it. I merely gave him a bit of bread."

Zel fed him? I know what feeding means. An animal fed comes back again and again. A man fed is no better.

"And I held Meta's head. . . ."

"Who is Meta?"

"His horse. I held her head while the smith took a tick from her ear. I did nothing. But the youth said he owed me something." Zel stops, lost in thought. She looks at me shyly.

I look away. I can tell from Zel's eyes that she has not told me something. The youth is already causing her to be furtive with me. Oh, how did so much happen so fast? Zel knows his horse's name. She tamed the beast. That youth must have been impressed with her. My blood swooshes, loud and insistent.

I close my eyes and dare to see what I fear in anticipation: The goose sits on but four lumps. She gets up now and checks them. I see the white and gray lumps. There is no doubt: rocks all! The goose has rolled the egg from the nest. My eyes search till they find it. This time the egg has cracked. The goose cannot raise another's child. The gosling is dead. This is the message the youth gave to Zel—as a gift. Despised gift. Cursèd youth. I would wring the goose's neck if I could. Oh, had I only left the goose tethered to her nest with the vine!

But geese are geese and people are people. How a goose behaves has nothing, less than nothing, to do with how people behave. Geese are stupid and smelly and hateful. Geese know nothing. Zel will realize this. Zel need not take the goose's message, the youth's message, to heart. I open my eyes.

"Mother, what is it?" Zel comes around the table and hugs me. "You look as though you would cry."

I pull my daughter onto my lap. "The world you know here, Zel, the world of our mountains and waterfalls, of our endless skies, do you love this world, Zel?"

Zel's head rises slightly higher than mine. I can't remember when she last sat on my lap. She presses my head to her and rests her chin on top. "How can you ask? You know I do."

I hug her. "Our alm is the best world imaginable." As the words leave my mouth, I regret their nakedness. I know in an instant that this is the moment I have dreaded. I must talk to Zel of the most important decision she will make in her life. I must give Zel the choice between a life with me forever and the ordinary life of stupid people who know no better. I must use the utmost care.

"Perhaps," Zel is saying slowly. "But I do love new places, new people."

I work hard to keep my arms from becoming iron like my teeth. As much as I would want to, I must not shackle Zel to me. I love her. That love must be returned freely. I cannot bear anything less. And I have a ready means of persuasion. Zel gave it to me yesterday when I made the cedar branch break and fall on the hedgehog. She wished for the gift of talking with animals. This desire resonates within her spirit. I speak with energy. I dangle the perfect hook. "If you could talk with animals, that would be much. You would give up certain things to have that gift, wouldn't you?"

Zel leans back so that she can look in my face. Her cheeks are red. Her eyes glow. "Oh, yes," she says in a half whisper.

I stroke her arms. "It would be worth choosing a life here in the country."

Zel smiles. "Choosing a life in the country is not giving up much, Mother."

I am encouraged. She is truly a mountain girl, unlike me. I dare to speak on. "It would be worth choosing a life without a husband."

Zel stiffens and sucks in air. I watch her eyes fight

pain. Then in an instant, her face clears. "Oh, Mother, I would never abandon you. You must stop thinking that at once. When I marry, I will take you with me." Zel claps her hands and laughs her relief. "We can all live together."

I swallow the bile that has risen to my tongue. I was mistaken; my daughter is not ready to choose. But that is no problem. There is time still. If I use enough skill and care, I will persuade Zel by the time her moon blood first flows.

I shut my eyes. The gosling is already deteriorating under the roasting sun. Ants have invaded the shell. The smell of rot attracts them. "Zel," I say, knowing now that I always knew I would eventually come to this lie, me, who has never allowed a lie to soil the air between myself and my blessed daughter, saddened by the unfairness of the price I have had to pay for this precious daughter, angry at that unholy price. "Zel, I must tell you a horrible thing."

Zel takes my hands. Her cheeks slacken. "What, Mother?"

I open my eyes. "Death would knock on our door."

"Death?" Zel squeezes my hands.

"Yes." I am amazed at the ease with which the lie comes. The ease exhausts me. Evil is heavy, indeed. "There are those who wish you ill, Zel. Who have always wished you ill."

"Mother!" Zel stands up. She looks around the room as though she would run away. "What are you saying?"

I know we must keep holding hands. "There are those who would push you from one of our cliffs, those who would kill you." I speak with a certainty not my own.

"Me?" Zel shakes her head. "But why, Mother?" Her words come out slowly, like stones rolling in wet grass. She shudders.

"We must protect you."

"Who wants such a thing? How do you know? Maybe I can talk to the person. I have done no harm." Zel frees her hands from mine. Frenzy lights her eyes. "You can come with me. Together we ..."

"Yes, together we can protect you." I stand. The pronouncement rises from my lungs, through my throat and mouth; yet I know what I say only as I hear it. "The gosling is dead."

"The gosling?" Zel stares at me. Then she runs to the window. The goose sits on her nest. Zel cannot see the egg, but I know she realizes I am right. I stand beside her and watch the tears move down her cheeks. "Tiny life, tiny bones." Zel presses her palm against her mouth. When she releases it, she turns to face me. Terror tightens her jaw. "What has the gosling to do with me, Mother?"

"You cannot take gifts people offer."

"I asked for the egg, Mother."

"But the youth insisted on giving you something."

My voice is so quiet, it is barely audible. "You must not be near people." My fingers take Zel's braids. "You will grow your golden hair." I speak without yet knowing where my words lead.

Zel twirls around. She raises her fists. "I don't see any sense to your words."

My confusion was equal to Zel's, but now it is past. I am already calling together the powers I know. They pulse in my veins, soak through my muscles. They tell me of a tower abandoned centuries ago. "A safe place. You will see."

Zel's tears stream now. They drop to her smock. They make dark circles over her breasts.

Chapter 9 ❖ Zel

urry, Mother," Zel whispers into Mother's ear. Did she just hear a cry behind them, an evil cry as of a hungry predator? The stalker comes. "Hurry."

Zel clings tighter. There is water all around. Water below them. Water that would suck them under, yet Mother races over it as though it is solid. Oh, merciful water that supports Mother's weight. Zel's feet do not touch the water. Her arms are wrapped firm around Mother's neck. Mother's cloak shields them both.

But Mother's cloak is not thick enough to ward off a dagger. Mother is stronger than Zel realized, for she carries her now without huffing and puffing. Still, Mother cannot fight off an enemy. "Flee faster, Mother."

Zel listens hard. She hears nothing but the slap of water on water. She dares to peek from the cloak upward. The sky is aglow with stars and a full moon. In this glow she and Mother must surely be visible to whoever follows. She shivers and ducks inside the cloak.

"Get down and run, Zel. But stay close." Mother is already racing along the shore. She scrabbles up the slope, pulling Zel by the hand.

An insect lands on Zel's cheek and crawls to her hair. She swats at it. It is so hard to keep up with Mother. Where did the woman's speed come from? And, oh, Zel is grateful for that speed. She uses all her strength to run. The pine branches scratch at her face. The forest is dense here. But that denseness is wonderful, for surely, oh, surely, it hides them.

And now Zel hears: Their running is loud. Twigs snap underfoot. They are as thunder. The stalker will have no trouble following them by sound alone. He needs no moonglow.

"Hurry, Mother."

But Mother stops. Zel yanks on her cloak. Then she sees. She swallows the scream in her throat. There before them looms a tower. Near the top are tall windows going clear up to the overhang of the roof.

Mother sits on the ground.

"What are you doing, Mother? Do you know this tower? Is this the safe place you spoke of back in the cottage?" Zel pulls on Mother's arm. "Get up. Oh, Mother, get up."

Mother sits, silent.

Zel looks around quickly. She sees no door into the tower. She races around the base. The door is on the far side. She pulls on it. She pulls and pulls with all her strength, but the wood does not budge. It is hard as stone. This must be the right place, but how will they get in? Zel rushes back to Mother and kneels beside her. "Mother, you must get up. We have to work together to open the door."

"Hush. Forget the door." Mother's eyes glitter hard in the moonlight. She stares beyond Zel at something. Something.

Zel spins around. The sapling walnut tree beside the tower, which was only half the height of the tower only moments ago, is growing, growing. It thickens and reaches; it grows. Zel cannot believe her eyes. She pants.

Mother stands and pushes Zel. "Climb. Fast. It is the only way in. Climb!"

Fear strengthens Zel's hands, makes her foothold sure. She goes from one thick branch to another, easily, as though this tree were made to have the branches at just the right distance apart for her legs. One branch leads directly to the wide window ledge of the tower. Zel jumps down inside and turns to help Mother into the room.

Her arms meet empty air. Mother isn't behind her.

"Mother!" Zel climbs back onto the window ledge.

But the walnut branch already retracts. It is too far from the window for Zel to reach.

Zel screams. "Mother!"

The tree is now shrunk to its normal height.

"Mother!"

Chapter 10 ❧ $\mathcal{M}$ otber

 put my fingers in my ears and run. I stumble. I hear Zel's scream still. I look for friendly ferns to stuff my ears, but the forest floor is covered with pine needles. I dig beneath them to the dirt and spit on dry grit. I plug my ears with the mud. And still I hear her scream. It is within my head.

I run to the shore. The water plants that rose beneath

my feet to form a path for us across the lake are still in place. It is deepest night; no one can be about at this hour. The risk that anyone will see me is small. And if someone does see, I'll dive and wait till he passes. He'll think it was his imagination. He'll forget it.

I cross the lake, walking from one plant to another. Once my foot hits the rocks on the other side, I close my eyes and see Zel, her back pressed against the side of the tower room, tears streaming down her face. She is safe. I check the door. The wood is petrified; it can never be moved. I have done well. Zel is safe.

The frenzy within me gradually subsides.

In its place comes a bitter taste. I saw Zel in my head only for an instant, yet I know the terror she chews now. My daughter is frightened beyond thought. Oh, if only I could comfort her.

A weariness far more thorough than any I've known before invades my bones. I must climb the hillside and return to the cottage for a good sleep. In the morning I must plant an extensive herb garden. I do not know yet why, just as I did not understand each task tonight until I found myself performing it.

I climb.

I stop and close my eyes. I see my daughter.

Zel is in the room. Her breath is loud as storm winds; her heart is loud as unripe fruit dropping from trees in those winds. She puts one hand over her mouth and the other over her heart. She presses. I know she strives to hush herself.

The tower room is utterly dark. Zel jerks as an owl hoots. She lifts her chin blindly toward an answering hoot. She shakes.

She dares to look outward over her shoulder. Shadows of bat wings cross at the top of the pines. Nothing else moves.

Slowly Zel slides one foot along the floor close to the wall. She pulls the other after it. She keeps her back to the tower wall and moves in this fashion the full circumference of the round room. She passes four windows in making the circle, ducking below each so that she cannot be seen from without. She keeps one hand on the cool stone of the wall behind her and the other hand stretched out in front toward the dark.

She stands immobile now, back leaning against the tower wall. Gradually, gradually the room becomes light. There is nothing in the room. Absolutely nothing. Stone walls, stone floor. But one stone is different. Zel kneels and touches.

It is a hatch. My heart contracts. I see the staircase leading down beneath it. Instantly I release energy into the wooden hatch. It hardens to stone, like the door at the base of the tower.

Zel digs at the edges of the hatch. She cannot lift it. No one can lift it. She works like a fiend. Finally, she slumps back on her heels. Then she crawls to beneath a window. She stands beside it, pressing herself against the wall, and peeks out. The predawn forest rustles. Animals scurry in the underbrush. The owl gives a victorious screech. Zel puts her fist in her mouth and bites down hard. Her eyes glisten. She breathes shallow and rapid. She lifts the edge of her smock and twists it. Her foot taps the floor silently, evenly. One two three four ... On and on.

I open my eyes. My daughter is as terrified as the rodent paralyzed in the owl's talons. I will not watch this.

I climb.

I stop again and close my eyes, but I refuse to see Zel. Instead, I check once more: The door is rock hard; the hatch is rock hard. Safe.

I climb.

Chapter 11 ❦ Konrad

 won't marry her." Konrad sits across the table from Father, his hands tense on his knees.

"You give me no explanation, yet you expect me to accept refusal. Your behavior is outrageous." Father's face is red again.

Konrad almost speaks Zel's name. But he stops himself. All he knows of the girl is her name, and a name is not an explanation. "I cannot marry this girl, this girl you found for me, Father. I cannot."

Father is silent for a moment. When he speaks again, his voice is changed. Konrad has seen him make this shift in public debates; he knows his father summons his powers of persuasion. "Listen well, Konrad. You told me you think of women now. Those thoughts have consequences, especially in these days of church reform. If you want a woman, Konrad, you must wed."

Konrad does want a woman. But he doesn't want this unknown wife, nor does he want a woman's attentions in exchange for money. "You don't understand."

Father stands, all semblance of patience gone. "I will not coddle any longer. Your refusal is intolerable!" He leans toward Konrad. "I have already made the pact, Konrad. Think of the strain on the relations between me and the girl's father. He is not just a duke, but a representative from his city-state to the highest legislature, the Diet of the Cantons. I am forced to see him regularly."

Konrad stands as well. "I cannot bend my life to meet the curves of your politics, Father."

Father's eyes bulge in anger. "Get out of my sight. And don't come back till you are ready to talk rationally."

But Konrad is already running, out the door, up the

stairs, to his room. He lies in bed and does not sleep, for the second night in a row. Konrad should marry this girl. Yet the thought of the wedding bed with the duke's daughter unnerves him. He argues with himself, taking first his father's side, then his own. And in the midst of the debate comes the image of Zel.

Konrad thinks of the moment at the smithy when he said he owed Zel something and she finally agreed that there was something she wanted. He would have given her double any sum she sought, just to show her she was ordinary. But she asked for a warm goose egg. And her request spun him around like a top.

How can he explain to Father that the thought of a girl who asks not for money but for a goose egg pushes all thoughts of other girls from his mind? Father would laugh. And with good reason. A chance encounter with a peasant girl. It is laughable.

But Konrad cannot laugh.

Like the speck of life in the fertilized goose egg, Zel entered Konrad's world and left a mark that changed him.

When Konrad rises the next morning, he pulls his clothes from the carved chests, snorting their woody smell, and runs down the stairs.

Father is closed in his accounting room.

Konrad eats and goes to his classics tutor. The poet

Ovid makes little sense today, though Konrad gives his best effort. Between Latin lesson and Greek lesson, Konrad seeks Father out. He will bargain for time somehow. He holds his voice steady. "I am ready to talk rationally."

"Good. I will send word telling them to set the date."

Konrad flinches. "It is irrational to set the date for a wedding that cannot take place."

Father stares at Konrad. "Do your lessons teach you nothing?" He shakes his head in disgust. "Leave me. Now."

Konrad cannot concentrate through the rest of his lessons, nor through jousting practice. He sits at last at the midday meal, elbows on the table, hands in his hair. His head feels as though it would explode.

Father enters and sits as well.

Konrad waits with dread for the pronouncement he knows must come. But his mother speaks first. "I consulted the stars last night." Her quiet voice dominates the room. "It is destined for Konrad to make his own choice."

Father wants to argue; it shows in his face. But he will not argue with the stars. In his view and in the view of most of the people Konrad knows, the stars determine plantings and harvests, trading and exploring, even conceptions and deaths.

Konrad views the reading of the stars with skepticism,

and his parents know that. He studies the work of Copernicus, and he agrees with that Polish-Prussian scholar that every bit of evidence suggests the sun doesn't circle the earth, but vice versa. So the organization of the universe may be entirely different from what his parents think—and their reading of the stars may be hopelessly flawed, even if there be merit to the notion of reading the stars. Still, he sits silent now, content to reap the unexpected benefit of his parents' beliefs.

Father's eyes study Konrad. It is clear he doesn't miss the irony of the situation. All the same, he cannot argue. The stars guide life. And, by Father's own admission, Konrad's mother reads the constellations better than anyone. It was she who stopped Father from traveling under the new moon one spring, thus sparing him the terrible hailstorm that fell on Stuhlingen.

Father sighs. "I will tell the young duchess's family that you aren't yet ready for marriage." Father drinks from his mug. He speaks with deliberation. "I will tell them I'll return in a year to discuss the matter further."

"I will never marry her."

"You'll come with me in a year." Stubbornness strengthens Father's voice. "You'll meet her." He looks to the countess, then back to Konrad.

A year, which has always seemed a long time to Konrad, now seems like almost nothing. For his Zel is young.

In a year will she be ready for ... for what? Konrad will not allow himself to think of what. He doesn't know the girl at all. Perhaps if he talks to her a second time, they will be bored with each other. Still, he cannot agree to Father's plan. He cannot think of any other girl. "Not in a year, Father. No."

Father rises from his chair, apoplectic.

"Tell them two years." His mother sips her wine and speaks with a steady, low voice. "In two years if Konrad has not found a wife of his own and if this young duchess is still unmarried, then Konrad will come with you to meet her."

Konrad waits, breath abated. Two years, please let Father give two years.

Father sinks to his chair in defeat.

The next day Father rides away, a scowl on his face, muttering about how the celebrations for Konrad's birthday, which is only on the morrow, will have to be delayed until he returns, and it serves Konrad right.

Konrad mounts Meta at the same time and goes directly back to the smithy. After all, he left the smith with an order to get information—the smith should have completed the task by now. "Where does Zel live?"

The smith blinks. Perhaps he thought Konrad wasn't coming back. He speaks slowly, like a half-wit. "Outside town."

"Where outside town?"

The smith shakes his head. "That I don't know, sire. I just know she's not a town girl."

"Anyone could tell she wasn't a town girl just from looking at her."

The smith stares at Konrad.

Konrad looks down. He sees he is pulling on one finger after the other. He stills himself. "Does she live on a farm or in a mountain cabin?"

The smith shakes his head again. "I don't know, sire. I asked around. No one knows anything about her."

"Think. There must be something you know." Konrad takes a coin from his pouch. "Anything."

"She has no oxen or donkeys."

Konrad is surprised. How can the smith have learned this if no one knows of the girl? "Tell me more."

"She has goats and chickens."

Now Konrad doubts the smith. But the man appears to have no spunk. He wouldn't dare tease a count. "What else?"

"I can't think of anything else, sire."

Konrad gives the smith the coin. Optimism stirs gently within him. The smith said they had no cart with oxen, no donkey even. So all their provisions had to be carried on their own backs. Surely that means they walked only a short way.

Konrad looks up at the clear sky. It bodes well. He

will start the search immediately. And at that determination, energy surges through him. He must begin.

But first Konrad returns to the castle, dismounts, and races to the study. His geography tutor has spread out a map in anticipation of the lesson. Beside the map is a chessboard with pieces at the ready—a treat to follow the lesson, no doubt.

The tutor beams and hugs a sheaf of papers to his barrel chest. "New reports from missionaries."

Konrad nods at the excitement in his voice. Reports from missionaries, navigators, land travelers—these are filled with amazing discoveries. Normally Konrad would be reaching for the papers eagerly, for he plans to travel himself someday. But this moment is not a normal moment. "I can't stay. We have to put geography off."

The tutor looks stunned. "I thought you were fascinated by the New World, which seems to grow every month."

"I am. Oh, I am." But right now other fascinations pull, fascinations this studious tutor might not understand, fascinations Konrad would not have believed possible just days ago. "We can discuss it all tomorrow."

"Tomorrow's your birthday."

Konrad laughs. How could he have forgotten? "Well, then, another day." And Konrad races back outside and mounts Meta.

He rides to the closest slope and stops at the first

home. A woman sits outdoors in the shade mending clothes. "Excuse me, madam. I seek information on a girl by the name of Zel."

The woman shakes her head. "I don't know of any Zel. But you could try the farm down the road there. They have plenty of people coming and going." The woman points. "Could be they've heard of her."

"Thank you."

Konrad goes directly to the farm and makes his inquiries. To no avail. He mounts once more and rides beyond into a valley and across more slopes, stopping at each dwelling. The people want to be helpful. But they know nothing. He speaks to a gaggle of women washing laundry at the lake edge. Each has suggestions. He goes to bed that night with a plan: The next day he will send three servants to gaily painted farmhouses with adjoining barns. They will cover the land.

Konrad sleeps well, finally.

The next morning is his birthday, and he wakes with unusual energy. He will resume the search himself. Why not? But first he must check with that dolt of a smith.

When he rides up on Meta, the smith comes running. "I remembered two more things, sire."

Konrad's hands tighten on the reins. "Speak."

The smith holds out his hand.

Konrad drops in a coin.

"Two things, sire."

Konrad drops in a second coin.

"First, she won't be back to market till winter, and she'll give me a visit when she comes then."

This is important news. This might mean the girl came from quite far away, after all. "And the second thing?"

"Today's her birthday."

"What? Today? Are you sure?"

"July sixth it is, isn't it, sire? Her mother was out getting presents for her birthday and putting them in a cloth sack. That she was. July sixth, the girl told me. Today."

Konrad's mouth has gone dry. Zel and he share the same birthday. Surely she isn't turning fifteen. She has to be at least two or three years younger than he is. So they weren't born on exactly the same day. The year differed. Still, the date is important. They are connected, oh, yes, Zel and Konrad are connected by the movement of the moon, by the changes of the sky and of the world's waters, by time itself. Zel and Konrad were born under the same star.

Goosebumps spread up Konrad's arms, across his chest.

He searches all that day and the next and the next. He rides week after week. He goes alone, because now the thought of being helped irritates him.

Daily he stops in at the smithy to see if anything has jogged the man's memory. But the smith is thick as a tree.

And the people whose homes he visits are hardly better. The further he goes from town and the more isolated the home he visits, the more the people answer brusquely. Some suspect he might want the girl for low purposes. They hesitate. He throws himself on their mercy, doing nothing to hide his own confusion at his growing need. Soon the tongues of even the most suspicious farm wives loosen. But the answers are the same. No one anywhere has heard of a girl with deep, dark eyes; yellow braids; a simple smock; a special way with horses; a cheerless mother (as the smith once described her to Konrad); and the name of Zel.

Yet she'll be back to the market in winter.

Konrad won't wait for winter. He can't. And, anyway, how could a girl and her mother make their way into town when the roads become ice slicks? The smith must have misunderstood. She'll be back soon.

Now even Konrad's dreams turn to Zel. He sees himself riding through an orchard and finding Zel perched in a tree. She tosses an apple core on his head and laughs. One leg dangles, uncovered by her smock—though she does not realize this—smooth and hairless as the tree bark. In another dream he's been riding all day. Meta stops to drink at a mountain pool. Konrad strips and jumps into the bracing water. And along comes Zel, cooing, luring the mare away with an early fall apple. She is unaware that Konrad's clothes are tucked in a bag hanging from the saddle. Naturally he has to fetch the mare back.

Dreams. In Konrad's dreams Zel has all the strength of the girl who dared to undo the lip rope at the smithy and hold Meta's head by herself. More even. She is modest but not hesitant. She laughs at his bumblings and he thrills to that laugh. But dreams lead nowhere. Konrad gnashes his teeth in his sleep.

Then one day, on the fifth week, the smith remembers another, final detail. "She loves lettuce."

"Lettuce?" Konrad at this point is willing to follow any lead. But lettuce? "How do you know?"

"Her mother said so."

Konrad pulls on his fingers, rubs at the back of his neck. "What exactly did her mother say?"

"She said, 'Let's go buy that lettuce you love.' " He holds out his hand. "Lettuce, sire."

Konrad puts a coin in the smith's hand. Lettuce isn't much to go on. Almost every farmer hereabouts grows lettuce and sells it in the market. But if the girl lives in the country, surely she grows lettuce in her own garden. So it has to be that the lettuce she loves is somehow special. And the mother said "that lettuce," so it isn't just any old lettuce. All right, Konrad will go to every lettuce vendor in the market until he finds the one with the special lettuce that Zel and her mother bought.

Amazingly, a man with only a few lettuce bundles and even fewer teeth claims to remember Zel. "A gentle girl with a winning way. I yank on her braids and she laughs." He gives an almost toothless grin. "Stupid girls are afraid of me, but not her." He shakes his head. "She comes to me every summer and buys this." He holds out a bunch of small, round lettuce leaves. "You can buy it. And pay once again over for the information."

Konrad looks at the plain, flat leaves. Why would Zel think these leaves are special? The farmer is probably making it up so he can have the money. "What makes you remember her so well?"

"Her smile. She never came without it."

Konrad remembers Zel's smile and its effect on him.

"And her eyes."

Zel's penetrating eyes, which appear in Konrad's dreams. "How do you remember that it was precisely this type of lettuce?"

"Ah, that's easy. Two ways." The farmer leans toward Konrad. "First, she asks for this lettuce in early July, but it grows best in the spring. I'm the only one around who grows it all summer." He looks proud of himself, as though he's waiting for Konrad to praise his wisdom in business matters.

Konrad's patience is tested. "The second reason?"

"The girl's name and the lettuce's name are the same."

Konrad rubs at his lower lip. "Her name is Zel."

"Her name is Rapunzel." The farmer shakes the bunch of leaves before Konrad's face. "I grow the best rapunzel around. Where's your money?"

Konrad pushes the lettuce away from his face with indignation. "I am Count Konrad."

"So you can afford it, then." The farmer smiles.

Konrad laughs in spite of himself. He wonders for a moment if this farmer and the boy at the goose farm who treated him so rudely are related. He drops a coin in the well-pleased farmer's hand.

That night he eats rapunzel with oil and vinegar. The next night he eats rapunzel with onions and tomatoes. He has rapunzel with boiled potatoes and rapunzel with strong cheese. Rapunzel with pork and rapunzel with perch. And rapunzel plain. Every day Konrad searches for Rapunzel. And every night Konrad feasts on rapunzel. The farmer comes to expect him in the market early. He saves his biggest, best bunches of rapunzel for Konrad.

But knowing her full name doesn't help any more than knowing her nickname. For no one Konrad asks knows any more about a Rapunzel than they know about a Zel.

Rapunzel, Rapunzel, where have you gone?

LONELY

Chapter 12 ❖ Zel

el leans out the south window. The stone is cold, but the sun has melted off the frost. She has just used the slop bucket and pushed it to the north side so she can escape the odor. The top of a lone spruce moves in the distance; a rogue bear scratches its back against the trunk. Perhaps he will pass this way. If Zel is lucky.

Zel has lived in this tower exactly one hundred days. Mother carried up the hay for her mattress and covered it with a single sheet embroidered in vine leaves.

Zel insisted on hay for her mattress, not straw, because hay smells sweet. And hay is what horses eat. Zel remembers the horse at the smithy, the smooth coat on the mare's back and the dark splotches on her thin, fine legs. She remembers the youth, how he looked at her. In her sleep she sees him eating the bread she gave him. Sometimes she is overcome with the urge to touch his dimple, just lightly, with one fingertip.

Her nights on that mattress are never peaceful. She misses being lulled to sleep by the fiddle. She misses

Mother's cool kiss and the rabbits' thick fur and the goats' nipping and butting. She misses climbing high until her throat aches in the cool, dry air and stepping barefoot from slippery rock to slippery rock in icy streams. She misses dirt, leaves, rain in her upturned face. Oh, she misses so much.

Zel pushes up her left sleeve. She holds her arm out and tilts it until her fine gold hairs catch the weak sunlight. She counts the hairs from wristbone to elbow. Sometimes she sits back on her heels and rocks as she counts.

She knows many numbers. The number of stones that make up the floor of this tower room: forty-four. Large and smooth. The number of days in this tower. One hundred days are many.

Zel stands in her birthday dress. Mother has explained that she chose green for hope. Zel is hopeful. Mother will conquer the threat outside. Or Zel will conquer it herself. She makes a fist. Zel is a fighter. But she'd rather not fight alone.

Mother will be here at noon.

If only Zel could tell time from the sky. But the sky changes with the seasons and the wind. Right there, for instance, just moments ago that cloud was flat on the bottom and lacy on top. But now the cloud has formed into lumps, and Zel predicts that a breeze will soon scatter the lumps. What reward can she give herself if she's right? Oh, she can get Mother to massage her neck. Her neck hurts these days from the weight of her hair, which grows unnaturally quickly. Every day she can see how much longer it is; she can feel how much heavier it is. She has asked Mother to cut it, but Mother says her hair will come in handy. When Zel asks what for, Mother doesn't answer.

Zel lies down on the hay mattress to rest her tired neck. She folds her hands on her chest. Now she can see nothing but her tower room, and that is the worst pain of all. She looks at her folded hands. She smiles. Her hands make drawings and paintings that confound her. Zel feels mystery enter her body, as though she harbors secrets even she cannot be allowed to know. Her bones grow heavy; they would merge with the stone of the tower if she stayed still too long. These thoughts alarm her; she does not recognize the girl who thinks them. She sits up suddenly, her back straight as a pine.

Most mornings Zel paints. When it was still summer, she painted the orange poppies, the yellow ranunculus, the blue gentian. She propped her paintings up along the bottom of the walls, as if they grew there.

Now, in early fall, she paints the greens and blues of the spruce, the browns of the occasional passing bear, the spotted yellows of the leaves that clutter the ground.

Mother gave her these paints. Generous Mother. Zel rises and takes a sheet of paper from the stack. She lays it on the window ledge. "What would you like painted on you today?"

A squirrel chatters from the walnut tree. Zel laughs. He flicks his tail, bushy thick for the approaching winter. "Don't go away. Please." Zel goes to her mattress and grabs the roll from her breakfast package. She rushes back to the window.

Zel pinches the inner part from the roll. She shapes it in the form of a walnut. "A delicious nut just for you." She tosses the dough pellet. It hits the tree below the squirrel. The squirrel darts upward, then stops, paws extended, skin stretched out in two arcs on each side. He chatters shrilly. The creature is angry at her. Ha! Zel takes another pinchful, squeezes it into a berry shape this time. "Look. A mulberry." She tosses, and it hits the squirrel on the back. The animal races around to the other side of the tree.

"Rascal." Zel laughs. She jerks her chin forward and cocks her head, just like the squirrel did. "You are better than the racing marmots and the stiff-bristled boars and the nervous hares. When I call to them, no matter how sweetly, they scurry into the underbrush. You are much, much better." Zel whistles.

The squirrel peeks out.

"And you are better than blackbirds and larks. They ignore my whistles—or, at most, glide for a wingbeat or two." Zel whistles and whistles and whistles.

The squirrel comes around to the close side of the trunk.

Zel puts her elbows on the ledge and leans forward. Her feet dangle under her. "Rascal," she sings out. Her voice is clear as mountain water. "Talk to me."

The squirrel darts around to the rear of the trunk again.

"Rascal," sings Zel. "Rascal, Rascal, Rascal."

And still the squirrel is absent.

Zel is alone. For one moment she had company. Now she is alone again. Alone and alone and alone.

"Coward!" Zel realizes she has shouted. Her pulse beats in her neck. She has shouted many times, shouted until she lost her voice—and never without fear. For her enemy could do terrible things if he found her.

Zel has gone over every moment she's ever spent with people other than Mother. Every moment of her life that she remembers. Oh, she lured a straying cow onto their alm once, just so she could talk with the herd boy. But he wasn't angry. He even told her stories. And she once stole a piece of wood the handyman's son had been whittling on. But after he gave her the cave rock, she managed to slip the wood back into the handyman's cart. He never even knew she stole it or he wouldn't have given her the cave rock.

No one anywhere should harbor ill will toward Zel. No one anywhere has Zel harmed.

So who is this terrible enemy?

Zel shouts again: "Come into view, coward enemy!" A bush at the base of a pine rustles. "I'm ready for you!" Zel points at the bush.

The wind rises. The bush moves, as do all the other bushes, as do the trees.

A flash of black and a birdcall. It is musical, not the harsh caw of a crow. It sounds like the chough, the highest flier of the Alps. What would that sublime bird be doing so low? In her wanderings above the tree line Zel has watched choughs ride the wind upward, then suddenly tumble and twist and somersault for the pure joy of it. The call of the rare bird now feels like a beckoning.

The urge to run grips her. "I am a mountain girl. I need the open." She makes the Jauchzer, the modulated yell common to the people of her mountains. She learned by mimicking the herd boys.

Zel hears no responding Jauchzer. Incipient panic burns her eyes. She needs responses.

She looks at the shrunken walnut branches. If they would only stretch out to her, she could coax the squirrel into her room the next time it comes around. But Zel cannot make the walnut grow like Mother can. Mother has a way with plants, an amazing, powerful way.

And Mother says that Zel will have a way with animals when she is ready. She says Zel will be able to talk with animals. Zel longs for that.

She dips her brush and paints the squirrel nibbling furiously at a dough pellet. The tail is poised for flight. Zel paints an ear, each hair separate, coming to a single sharp point.

Chapter 13 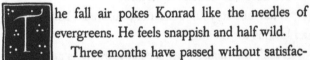 Konrad

The fall air pokes Konrad like the needles of evergreens. He feels snappish and half wild.

Three months have passed without satisfaction. But at least they have passed without interference from his parents. The changing church took care of that. The church police have been busy purging the town. They strip altars, they smash organs, they break the stained-glass windows. The count and countess spend their time trying to ease confrontations between the old church and the new.

But this reprieve from his parents' interference had to come to an end sooner or later. So today, when Konrad comes downstairs to find his mother awaiting him in the dark of pre-morning, he is not surprised.

The countess stands with hands stretched toward him. "Tell me, Konrad. What ails you?"

"Nothing, Mother."

"Your pain shows in every move." Her voice catches.

Konrad cannot bring himself to say Zel's name. But his heart responds to his mother's sincere entreaty. "I'm looking for something."

"What? Let us help you."

Konrad shakes his head.

The countess lowers her chin and looks up at Konrad with eyes that implore. "And this search matters so much that everything else must be forgotten?"

"Nothing else matters right now."

"What about your education, Konrad? You haven't had lessons for months."

"Didn't the minister say secular learning is an insolent conceit?"

The countess takes a step backward. She looks amazed. "You've never quoted the clergy before."

Konrad gives a sheepish smile. "He said something useful for once."

"Useful to him, not to you." Her disdain shows in her tone. She looks around the room quickly and moves closer. "Speak your own mind, Konrad." The countess puts her hand on Konrad's arm. "What do you search for with such frenzy?"

"I can't talk sensibly about it." Konrad swallows the lump in his throat. "I don't seem to understand anything."

"That's hard for me to believe of the youth who rattles off mathematical formulas, making his tutors rejoice. You can do anything you put your mind to, Konrad."

Konrad gives a small laugh. He wishes it were that simple.

"I'm worried for you."

"Youths my age take up arms for pay to fight in foreign wars. All I do is ride through the countryside. There is nothing to worry about."

"There might be." The countess tightens her grip on Konrad's arm. "One night this August I saw the constellation of Perseus burst into a shower of comets."

"What does Perseus have to do with me?"

"He is the great horseman. He rides Pegasus. Please, Konrad, though you have your doubts, respect my beliefs. Even medical students study astrology. As you ride under the evening skies, watch Perseus. If that was a warning, you must heed it."

Konrad puts his hand over his mother's. "I'll take care of myself."

"It is not yet fully light out. Check the skies now." Her tone is urgent. "Check them every morning. Every evening."

Konrad kisses his mother's cheek. He ascends the stairs and throws open the doors of his balcony to the blast of icy air. The sky shows no stars. But maybe Konrad needs to be higher to see them. He jumps onto the balcony ledge and climbs over the low roof. He swings himself onto an upper walkway, takes the stairs at a run, and he is in one of the four turrets. The sky is empty and pure.

Konrad looks out across earliest morning on the lake. He tingles with anticipation. Though he cares little for the talk of Perseus, he feels strengthened by his mother's belief in him. He races down the steps and outside.

Konrad picks up a stiff-bristle brush and enters the paddock. The mare greets him. He brushes her well. Then he presses his cheek against the mare's neck. She whinnies with a hesitant gentleness.

Konrad thinks again, for the thousandth time perhaps, of how Meta pressed against Zel's new breasts. The peasant girl should have been coarse as her bread, yet she was tenuous as a memory. She was not pretty. Still, there was something oddly pleasing about her looks. Will she recognize him when next they meet? Konrad saddles Meta and mounts.

"Young sire." Annette runs from the kitchen. She holds up a sack to Konrad. "The countess had me pack you a hearty meal."

"With much thanks." Konrad takes the sack and leaves. He follows the road south, his eyes on the changing leaves of hardwoods scattered among the pines. The colors recall the oranges and blues of the frescoes in the church belfry. The forest evokes reverence. He goes hushed and slow, until Meta finally announces her needs in a loud whinny. He eats by the lakeside. Meta nibbles on the dry grasses and drinks fully. Konrad, too, puts his face to the lake and drinks. Then he leads Meta by the reins into the woods. He uses his teeth to pull the cork from the bottle. He drinks as he walks. Then he recorks the bottle.

He goes all day. Darkness falls. The trees huddle together, almost as though they fend off the moonlight.

Hunger begins as an annoyance. His parents will be worrying about him by now. He mounts Meta, and the horse breaks into a trot. A branch catches Konrad's sleeve and rips it like a claw shredding a spider web. He turns to look at it, and another branch knocks him from the saddle.

Konrad hits the ground, shoulder first. On impact he rolls instinctively. He slams against a tree trunk. He rubs his face with both hands. He feels a disorientation so pervasive he fears he is lost for good. He whistles to Meta and mounts again. He fights the urge to return home.

Konrad gives the horse free rein, for with this blackness he cannot guide her anyway. As legend goes, souls who are neither folded into heaven nor banished into hell wander the Alps at night and pass by to touch the warm hands of sleepers. Konrad clenches his hands inside his pockets and shivers.

They emerge from the forest suddenly, to find themselves on a cliff edge over the lake. Konrad grabs the reins just in time. His heart pounds. Even in the weak light of the stars, the rocks at the lake shore far below glisten. Konrad walks Meta with care. At the first thinning of the trees, he turns the horse inward and upward again.

They reach a small clearing. Konrad dismounts and drinks from the bottle of wine.

Konrad wakes. The ground is hard and so wet that his shirt is soaked. A stick is jammed against his thigh. He sits up with a start. He senses a whir. Bats cut the weak moonlight at the top of the trees. Pine resin soaks the air. Now he remembers: He slipped off Meta to rest, and he must have slept. It is still night, though the night is no longer deep. He rubs his hands together to dispel the chill.

His mouth is dry. He gropes for the bottle. It is empty. And his shirt stinks of wine. He must have spilled it on himself when he fell asleep.

He puts his lips together to whistle to Meta, but they are soft and puffy, and all that comes is a light whoosh. Still, the mare knows. She trots over and nuzzles Konrad's face. He mounts.

Konrad licks his lips and listens hard for sounds of running water. These mountains are rich with streams. And there's the telltale song now. They come to a small wooden bridge. Konrad dismounts, and horse and man drink.

As the beginnings of dawn steal the stars, Konrad discerns a path down the mountainside, the direction he must go to return home. He prepares to take the path when he sees a goose.

The goose is settled on a strong-looking, high-sided nest. Konrad looks around for the rest of the flock. But this goose appears to be a loner. His groggy brain slowly sees the contradiction: The goose sits on a nest, but wild broods hatched months ago. Konrad learned that lesson only too well when he went in search of the hot goose egg for Zel.

The goose gets off the nest and wanders in the dirt, pecking at nothing, it seems. Konrad walks toward the exposed eggs. He counts five. But there is something odd about them. They vary much in size and shape. Konrad steps closer. They are stones!

The fast, high cry of a fiddle cuts the air. Konrad spies a cottage. A cock crows from somewhere behind the home. The air tastes of goat. Cypresses stand tall on the far side of the alm.

The fiddle keens with clarity. It makes his flesh tighten. If he listens much longer, he will be unable to hold back tears.

Konrad has become unused to hearing secular music—no lyres, no fifes, no fiddles in the town square anymore. This fiddler either does not know of the ban or does not care.

The music shocks Konrad, for the anguish it speaks is thorough. This fiddler is without hope, without salvation. Rapunzel cannot live in a home wracked with misery. Yet Konrad is here now, and he has come very far to get here.

He walks to the cottage.

Chapter 14 ❖ *Mother*

The music uses my chest as a sounding board. My hand grips the warm maple neck of this fiddle. My fingers press strong on the strings. They hold the bow tight. They pull the bow hard across those sheep-gut strings, hard and long, all the way to the tip of the bow. My chin grows out of the top, as much a part of the instrument as the bridge. I feel the vibrations in my cheek. I am the fiddle. I am the bow.

The notes pat the fuzz of hair on my skin. They are breath. They make me know there is still rhythm to this existence.

The morning light is watery today. It slides around

the room, edging into corners, soaking the bottoms of chair legs, table legs. It enters the fiddle through my open mouth and closed eyes. It heats me, the wood of me, the sheep gut of me, the flesh and water of me. It insists.

Knock knock.

I open my eyes and stand. I set the fiddle in its spot on the shelf. I rest the bow beside it. These hands ache from the sudden, brutal lack of the fiddle. I straighten them, extending my fingers taut.

Knock knock.

Visitors are rare. I open to a bedraggled youth who reeks of sour wine. His clothes show wealth, but one sleeve is ripped and his eyes carry the weight of lost sleep. I feel his disorientation. He is not drunk, despite the stench. His demeanor touches me. "Have you lost your way?"

"I think I have." The man's eyes try to wander past me into the room. "Was that you playing the fiddle?"

How long was he listening? And why? "I scratch out a few notes now and then."

"Never fear. I won't report to the church police. I also love music."

The church police? The words sound ridiculous on this isolated alm. I fear no forces of the Lord. I take no part in the petty struggles of society. I nod, purely to hurry him along.

"Do you have a family?"

I stand tall. There is nothing aggressive in the man's posture, but his question is bold. A woman is always at risk.

"I don't mean to alarm you." He speaks quickly and with a gentle tone. "I was looking for a family."

Ah. So he stumbled across this alm by accident. Good. I hold the edge of the door, ready to close. "I live here alone."

He hesitates. "Could I ask you a strange question?"

His eyes are now childlike. I could never refuse a child. I cross my arms at the chest. "Ask."

"I was wondering about that goose."

That wretched goose that stays though others have already migrated south. "Go ahead, kill her. Take her home and eat her."

The man steps back as though surprised. "Well, she's sitting on a nest and . . ."

"Kill her."

I close the door and close my ears. I will not listen for the sounds of the man killing the goose. Let her simply disappear. I stand in one spot for a long time. Long enough for our alm to be empty of the stranger.

My fingers reach out again into the morning air. If I could rip the sunlight away, wring it in my hands like laundry, I would. I want the night back. I can barely face another day of this.

But I mustn't curse the dawn. For Zel needs the light to draw by. She's doing very well. I mustn't despair. I can see progress already. She gets frustrated now and then. Of course she would. She'd like to be with me all the time, like before. Soon she'll realize that I am all she needs. That's when I can explain to her. Though I miss her more than blood itself, I can be patient.

The sunlight is weepy. This day calls for cheering up. An onion soup. The girl loves onion soup.

I go outside and pick my way through the garden. Some of the herbs are tendrils yet. I take care not to trample them. I pull a bunch of new onions. I lean over the herbs and whisper. They seem to shake off the morning frost and stretch, like fox cubs. I could make them grow outrageously, all the way to the sky. But I don't. I reserve my energy for the demands of visiting Zel. I pick a handful of tiny leaves.

The goose calls. The man left without killing her. She rises into the air, turns, and heads south. I have refused to look at her these past months. Now I need not turn my head away as I cross our small wooden bridge. I am glad to be rid of her.

Indeed, I want never to think of the cursèd goose. If it were not for the bird's insanity, Zel would not have asked the youth at the smithy for an egg. That youth would not have made an impression on her. He would not have encumbered her soul.

I walk swiftly toward the bridge. I put the herb leaves in one pocket and the onions in the other. I clench both fists. I go straight to the hateful nest of rocks. My feet kick wild deathblows. Twigs and feathers fly. And my feet suddenly fly, too. I feel sharp pain.

When I open my eyes again, I know that I was out cold. Much time has passed. I rise and touch the swollen mass behind my ear, where my head smacked the ground. I cannot linger. Zel expects me at noon. I notice hoofprints in the dirt. The man who came and went this morning was on horseback.

I hurry to the cottage, rotating my shoulders, working out the kinks from my fall. Dots circle before my eyes. A blackness comes, and I bend forward quickly. The nausea rises, then settles. My eyes clear again. I straighten and move more slowly.

Why didn't I smell horse on the man? Because he reeked of wine.

I set water to boil and drop in an egg. The beginnings of a worry scratch at the backs of my eyes. I peel onions. I choose three apricots, wash and dry them. I cut a chunk of fresh goat cheese. I cut an equal chunk of bread. I wrap all separately in paper, then fold them together in one supper bundle. A far cry from onion soup, but nonetheless nourishing.

I choose a ripe plum and a sweet roll. Didn't I give

her a plum just yesterday? I should have gone to the cellar and chosen an apple. But there's no time now. I wrap plum and bun in paper to make her breakfast bundle for tomorrow. The worry claws through to the front of my head. My eyes would split.

The boiled egg is ready. I peel it. I cut two slices of bread, cover them with the herbs from my pocket, and dice in the egg. Steam rises, coloring my hands. I wrap the hot food. I pack all into my cloth bag. Then I add the light slop bucket. It is clean and fresh.

My feet take the path down in little leaps. I go too fast to hold branches aside. They slap at face and arms. A branch catches my sleeve. I stop before it rips. I think of the ripped sleeve of the young man. The man in search of a family. The man who asked about the goose but didn't kill her. I know now I have seen him somewhere else. When? Oh, when, when? And finally it comes to me: He is the man who knocked the package from my hand the last time Zel and I were in town. The noble in a hurry. He was in town the same day Zel was in town. The worry shouts in my head. He was not drunk today, yet he carried the stench of wine. Could he have poured wine on himself to cover the smell of horse? Could he have deliberately deceived me?

I drop to my knees. I need energy for the long trek to visit Zel. Yet I cannot afford not to spend whatever energy it takes now to stop the danger. I close my eyes and raise my hands high above my head, and I command this whole forest. I command it to spin and twirl and change and change. I command it to reconfigure itself so that no one will recognize it ever again. So that no stranger can come twice to our alm.

Chapter 15 ❧ Konrad

he fiddle tune of the lone woman on the alm plays and replays in Konrad's head. He has to fight to keep it from lulling him into a sleep that on this precipitous, twisting path would mean sure death.

The woman who opened the door was dark-haired and hazel-eyed, almost the exact opposite of Rapunzel. She can have nothing to do with Rapunzel. Yet Konrad cannot put her out of his mind. When he asked about the goose, her face hardened; her cheeks glowed; she exuded urgency. About a goose. A goose that sits on rocks. The whole encounter was bizarre.

And the twisted endlessness of this path doesn't help. As long as Konrad goes downward, he cannot get truly lost. Yet his apprehension grows. The trees crowd in on both sides. They seem to close behind him, as though he's emerging from water. He squeezes his thighs and Meta breaks into an uncertain trot. The horse's ears pin back. Konrad feels sure the mare, too, has the sensation of racing before the tide.

It is evening when Konrad and Meta reach the castle. Konrad falls into bed. He awakens in the middle of the night and remembers the cock crowing and the smell of goat and the cottage on the alm.

He sits bolt upright. All at once he knows what he has seen—a goose with nothing but stones in her nest, a goose that would be very happy to receive the gift of a fertilized egg.

Rapunzel's goose.

Chapter 16 ❖ Zel

he branch of the walnut tree stretches toward Zel. "Mother," she calls in delight. "Mother, Mother."

Mother enters through the window. "Oh, my Zel."

They hug. The bulk of Mother inside her thick dress is solid and real and wonderful. Zel takes Mother's hands and holds them to her cheeks. She breathes the odor of onions. "Oh, if only I could stand in the kitchen beside you chopping onions." She nuzzles Mother's palms. "Stay longer today."

"As long as I can."

"Your hands are so cold, Mother. Frigid." Zel rubs Mother's hands. "What have you brought?" She moves so that her side is touching Mother's side. She reaches for the cloth sack. Zel opens the drawstring and takes out the clean slop bucket. She puts it down quickly and holds the first bundle of food to her nose. "What? From the smell of your hands I expected onions. But I don't recognize this other smell."

"There are onions in the dinner bundle." Mother smiles. "But lunch is herbs. Herbs to keep your hair growing."

Zel unwraps the two slabs of bread and opens them. Herbs deck a hard-boiled egg. She wants to pick them out and throw them away. "My hair is too long already. It grew again last night. Another toe's length."

"Good."

"Why? Why is that good, Mother?"

"You'll see."

Zel takes a corner of Mother's dress in her hand. "Your hem is wet. Did you walk on water to get here?"

Mother laughs. "I am not an insect, a water strider. I am not a water bird."

"Why is your hem wet then?"

Mother sits beside Zel on the floor. She lifts one of Zel's long braids onto her lap and unravels it carefully.

Zel listens to Mother's hard breath. Home must be very distant. Zel isn't sure where this tower is. Their journey here seemed endless—but time at night can be deceptive. Zel has learned from some of her sleepless, terror-filled nights in this tower how endless time at night can seem.

Still, even in the confusion of that night, Zel noticed things. She holds Mother's wet hem fast. "You did cross the lake today, didn't you? I remember crossing the lake with you, Mother, the night we came here. You walked on water. Do you have a special way with water like you do with plants?

Mother smoothes Zel's hair.

Zel yanks on Mother's skirt. "Tell me."

Mother clears her throat. "Don't talk foolishness. My hem is wet because I was careless near the lake, I was in such a hurry. Something delayed me, and if I didn't rush, I'd have been late."

"What delayed you?"

But Mother is busy again with Zel's hair. Mother has so little energy left, yet she never fails in the arduous task of caring for Zel's hair. "Poor Mother." Zel kisses Mother's hand.

Mother hums.

"I miss your fiddle. Won't you bring it next time you come? I want you to play for me as I go to sleep."

"It's hard enough for me to carry your provisions." Mother finishes unraveling the braid.

Zel holds the corner of Mother's skirt in one hand and picks up the bread and herbs in the other. She takes a bite. It's really very good. "Who teaches you about these new herbs?"

"No one."

But Zel noticed the slight wrinkle of Mother's nose when she asked the question. This question disturbs Mother. "Then how do you know which herbs will make my hair grow?"

"I just do." Mother combs Zel's loose hair. Her voice is hard. She may be angry.

"I miss you, Mother."

"I miss you more, Zel. I suffer more."

Suffering. Was it really only a few months ago that Zel hardly knew what suffering was? Her memory of herself on the day they went to market seems so childlike.

Zel thinks suddenly of the squirrel. Perhaps he ran to his wife when Mother came. "Mother, do animals have true love? I mean really true, like people do?"

Mother separates Zel's hair into three groups of precisely equal size. She starts the braid close to Zel's head, so tight it hurts. Zel yelps. But Mother braids uninterrupted.

Zel is seized with irritation at Mother's refusal to answer. She wants to argue, to shout. She looks past Mother at the tree.

The squirrel is nowhere in sight. Zel's only reliable company is Mother. The one slim daily hour with Mother is Zel's best treasure. She must be obedient and good, so Mother will come without fail. She calms herself.

Zel touches the egg in her lunch. "What has become of the goose?"

Mother's fingers move quickly as they braid. Her humming is faster now.

Zel feels tension in Mother's hands on her hair. Mother is always tense when Zel talks of the goose. Other things make Mother tense, also. Zel can't resist exercising her power to make Mother anxious. She is almost giddy as she speaks: "Mother, do horses know true love?"

Mother braids so fast, Zel is sure the hair will tangle. Yet it doesn't. Mother is a magician at braiding.

Zel clenches her jaw. She will make Mother respond. "Does the horse Meta know true love?"

"There's no point in thinking about that horse. Think about animals you haven't met yet, Zel. Think. . . ."

"I will never know other animals here in the tower. The one animal I can think of is Meta."

"Stop thinking about that boy and his horse!" Mother stands, and Zel's braid falls to the floor.

Zel looks out the window again. "The walnut tree is happy when its branches are full, as they are now."

Mother sits. She picks up the second braid. "Trees aren't happy or sad." Her voice strains with anger.

Zel cannot stop herself from licking the razor edge of challenge. "Yes, they are, Mother. The walnut tree wants to sing when it's big."

"No. I know about trees. I know about plants." Mother's fingers rip at Zel's braid as they unravel the hairs. "The tree must shrink in upon itself when I'm not here, Zel. Otherwise what would prevent your enemy from climbing up, just as I do?"

And what would prevent me from climbing down? But how can Zel think such a thing? Danger surrounds the tower. She must not forget. "Tell me about the enemy. Tell me everything you know, Mother."

"I've told you. He would kill you if he could."

"I don't see him, Mother. I see no trace of him. Sometimes I cringe in fear. But other times I'm sure he's not around. Nowhere near. At those times all I want is to leave this tower and run free again."

Mother's grip on Zel's braid hurts. Mother whispers, "You need to learn to think right, Zel. You need time to become reasonable." It is as though Mother speaks to Zel's thoughts—as though she knows Zel has truly considered climbing down the tree.

Has Mother seen inside Zel's head? Does Mother invade Zel's being? Anger flushes Zel's face. But no, she mustn't allow herself anger. She must listen to Mother.

Zel eats the rest of her bread. She wants to think right, to be reasonable. Suddenly the futility of Mother's actions strikes her. "By morning my hair will have grown, and the braids will be loose yet again."

"Tomorrow I will braid them anew, like always."

"When my hair grew at a normal rate, you only braided it once a fortnight. Don't you get tired of doing it every day?"

"I love braiding your hair. I have always loved it."

"Don't you get tired of searching for my enemy?"

"Never, Zel."

"I'm tired, Mother. I'm tired, and all I do is sit here and wait. You have to be, too."

"No. I must keep up my search tirelessly."

Zel wishes the faceless enemy would come while Mother is there. It would be a terrible fight and Mother would slay him. Oh! What a dreadful wish! Zel has never wished harm to anyone before. Zel leans forward and places her cheek on Mother's knee. "Stay today, Mother. Please."

"I can't, Zel."

"I get cold." Zel knows this is unfair to say. She manipulates Mother, for Mother cannot bear the thought of

Zel suffering physically. Zel is ashamed of her weakness of spirit. Yet her need forces her words. "The weather has changed. I get so cold. Take me home."

"I can't."

"Put me to bed in my own bed. Play your fiddle till I sleep."

"You know that's impossible."

"Then stay with me, Mother. Oh, stay."

"I must search for the enemy."

"Someday you will tire of looking for this enemy. You seem near exhaustion when you come."

"I will never tire of it, Zel. I will protect you forever."

The words chill Zel more than the fall winds, more than anything else Mother could have said.

Chapter 17 ❖ M o t h e r

 stand and leave quickly, through the window, down the tree. I wait while the tree recedes upon itself, until the tower is once more secure. Zel does not look from the window.

The girl's penchant for argument grows worse each day. I clench my hands on braids that are no longer there. Zel has luxurious hair. Her braids came firm and reliable under my weaving fingers. Zel's hair is strong as rope. I have a sudden urge to grab and twine it around my neck as though it were a noose. I think of the hair noose snapping my neck.

I am shocked at my own self-loathing. This emotion has no right to hold me. If I were to die, I'd leave Zel alone in this world. I must never do that. Never.

Zel would not be better off without me. She needs what I am doing.

What am I doing?

I'm preparing my daughter for the choice. There is no other way.

I sit on the ground. The nights have become cold. Yet I cannot allow Zel a hearth for warmth. Though there are no roads on this side of the lake, a hunter might spy a curl of smoke, even in this dense evergreen forest.

The thought of her shivering undoes me. I call upon the ground ivy. I entreat its thin stems. I coax and cajole. From all sides, ivy climbs the tower walls, growing, growing. A swelling tide of green that will hold in warmth, that will stop Zel's shivering. In winter the snow will catch on wide ivy leaves and blanket the tower further.

I pant as I survey my work. The ivy grows in such profusion that the stones of the tower are no longer seen. From a distance the tower appears as an evergreen tree.

Yes. I was worried about some stray person spying the tower now that leaves are falling. Two problems solved at once.

And should that youth stumble upon this green tower—that youth who didn't fool me, no, he never fooled me, for I saw the searching in his eyes, oh, yes, he must be searching for her now—should he grab at the ivy stems, they will come away in his hands, for they are thin, thin. His searching, his finding, all in vain. I would laugh at my own cleverness. But I do not have the energy. I swoon.

OBSESSED

Chapter 18 ❧ Konrad

onrad gets up from bed. He does not stop to eat or change his wine-soaked clothes. He is sure he can retrace his steps. Dawn will be upon him by the time he reaches the path that leads up the mountainside to the little wooden footbridge. He will stand before Rapunzel in broad daylight this very day.

But Konrad is wrong. The path eludes him. He knows it was right here. But it isn't. And, after all, he had missed almost a full night's sleep when he came across the alm, so maybe his memory is clouded. Maybe the path is a little more to the south. He searches. A little more to the north. He searches.

Konrad rides Meta up one wooded mountainside after another, his eyes alert for cypresses. Many times he ends up in lovely alms, but never in the right alm. Konrad rides till night and beyond, haunted by the fiddle tune. When morning comes, he keeps riding. Another day. Another night. Shadowy chasms drop away on either side.

Many times a path looks familiar, yes, he knows it precisely; then it turns out to lead nowhere. Konrad falls asleep on Meta's back and wakes to find himself in his own bed with his mother at his side.

"Awake at last, Konrad?"

"How did I get home?"

"Meta brought you."

Konrad pushes himself up on his elbows. "I have to go."

His mother pushes him back down with no effort at all. "You're not going anywhere. You need to eat and rest."

"I have to find a goose."

His mother's eyes narrow. "A goose?"

"A goose that sits on stones instead of eggs."

His mother's face is now guarded. She pats Konrad's hand. "I'll get you something to eat, Konrad. You stay in bed."

"And a girl."

"A girl?" The countess looks slightly hopeful. "Is that what this is all about?"

"Zel. That's her name."

"So you've fallen in love." The countess shakes her head ruefully. "And all along I've been so worried." She smiles. "Tell me about her."

"I met her at the smithy."

She nods. "She was having her horse shod?"

"She has no horse or cow or much of anything. She lives in a small cottage on an alm."

"She's a peasant girl." The countess stands up. "Now I know why you're miserable. This talk of marriage has disturbed you beyond reason. You need to eat. Then sleep. We can talk sensibly later."

The next day the countess comes to Konrad's room with the count. The count sits at the desk chair. The countess stands by Konrad's bed. Konrad tells his parents everything.

For once, Konrad's father sits silent.

The countess speaks up. "It's all harebrained. You know nothing of the girl, Konrad. By your own admission, she is a mystery to you."

"I know her spirit, Mother. It glows with boldness."

"Konrad, you and this girl have nothing in common. She has no education, no training, no refinement. . . ."

"Zel is refined!"

"The spirit of a peasant who tries to entice a count is neither refined nor bold, but insolent."

"She didn't try to entice me. She was bold enough to take charge when the smith looked in Meta's ear, that's all. And she was lighthearted enough to ask for a goose egg when she knew she could have asked for practical things. And . . ."

"Oh, Konrad, stop this. She's a peasant. You can't even imagine what she's really like."

Konrad swings his legs over the side of the bed and sits on the edge, ready to rise. "Aren't you the one who read the stars? I am to make my own decision."

"Here's what we'll do," says Father, suddenly standing.

"Yes, you tell him." The countess steps aside.

Konrad tenses for a fiercer fight.

"We will send out the manservants. They will find this cottage and bring back the maiden."

Konrad can hardly believe this turn of events. A smile breaks across his face.

The countess reaches out in protest. "But . . ."

The count cuts the countess off with a quick look. "And, Konrad, once she is here, you will return to your lessons and tasks. You will lead the life you led before, the life you were bred for, and you will see that this Zel has no place in that life." The count now turns to the countess. "He will learn for himself that she is unsuitable."

Zel is not unsuitable. Not by any measure. But Konrad sees that fighting the point is not in his best interest. The manservants will find Zel. That's what's important. "Yes, Father."

And so the manservants search for the cottage on the

alm. But they return empty-handed. Konrad sends them out again, and he goes with them this time. He is convinced that the fiddler has his Zel. And he is convinced something is very wrong. Perhaps the girl has fallen ill—she must have—for nothing less could account for the profound sadness of the woman's music.

They search day after day. Father decides that only one servant should accompany Konrad. So Konrad searches with that one servant for the rest of the month. Then even that man is needed elsewhere. Konrad searches alone again.

The fall ends. Winter rains, then ices, come. There is no point in trying to find a mountain path any longer, for such a path, were it found, would be impassable until spring.

Konrad goes to the smithy every day. "Send for me immediately if the girl appears." The same demand every day.

"You know I will, sire." The same response.

"There is a heavy purse involved."

The smith nods.

Konrad resumes his lessons now. He studies alchemy to be able to judge the purity of goods, for Father has put him in charge of the town's growing commerce. One of his major responsibilities is to thwart would-be cheaters. Konrad scoops the spices from their damp vaults and dries them before weighing. He tests for brick dust added to the medicinal Sumatran ginger. Trickery abounds, but he is diligent.

Konrad guards against dangers as well. He cuts away the toxic leaves from the New World rhubarb before repacking it for the surgeons. He checks for eggs, parasites, cocoons in the guaiac wood brought from the West Indies to treat syphilis. No caterpillars will ruin their crops, like the scourge of Troyes. No small monster will sneak in on cloves from the Moluccas.

Still, Konrad steals time to ask in town after a girl with light braids and dark eyes who goes by the name of Rapunzel. And most Saturdays and every Sunday he rides as far up the mountainsides as the ice permits. With the arrival of spring, Konrad wakes before dawn to fit in a daily visit to the smith before haggling with the importers. He takes to eating the midday meal rapidly, so he can fit in a visit to the rapunzel vendor, as well, before he's expected back at work.

And he buys great quantities of the lettuce.

Annette watches him. "I think you grow rabbit whiskers, young sire."

Konrad twitches his nose at her.

After spring comes summer, with his birthday and Zel's birthday. July sixth. A day sacred to Konrad. He drinks much wine and falls asleep under the stars, thinking only one thought: The universe has conspired to bring Zel into his life, and all he can do is surrender to the awesome power.

Then comes fall. Winter. Spring again.

Konrad stands on his bedroom balcony. He rubs his arms, though there is no chill in the air. He covers his mouth and nose with both hands and breathes his own warmth. The taste of despair coats his tongue. Spring is too cruel.

Chapter 19 ❖ *M o t h e r*

 sit at the table. I think of the food I should prepare for dinner, but I do not move. I sit and look at nothing.

I don't have to see nothing. I have the choice of seeing whatever I want. Whomever I want. But I see nothing.

I think of a story.

Once upon a time there was a little girl full of all the whimsy and unspoken hopes of any little girl.

The girl married a boy she half-fancied and waited for the children to come. She waited and waited and waited. Her mother, who had had eleven children if the stillborn ones were counted, and the girl counted them, waited with her. After a while her mother died, still young, but worn. Waiting grew bitter. Her husband, the boy-now-man, wouldn't wait any longer. Or maybe he was tired of watching her wait. He left.

The girl-now-woman went about her business. But she couldn't stop herself from noticing all the babies of the world, none of whom would ever call her Mother.

At first she tried helping. She tended the babies, to give their mothers a break. She became expert on the fiddle her mother had left her, and the little ones danced to her music. She kissed them and cuddled them and worked to make her fingers release them when their mothers came for them. She tried.

But she couldn't keep herself from envy. She couldn't help despising her own body.

The woman was a good person. She didn't want to covet the round bellies of the women who used to be her playmates just a half-dozen years ago. She didn't want to chew the insides of her cheeks at the sight of her own sisters pregnant. She knew she could serve God simply by living a good life; she didn't need to be Mother to be valuable.

Yet she needed to be Mother. She looked in other women's flat faces and saw that they either had children or, in a few cases, didn't. It was a simple bit of information in their eyes. No one else seemed hounded with need. But the woman needed, oh, how she needed, to be

Mother. She needed it with every drop of blood, every bit of flesh, every hair, every breath of her body.

The woman took to staying at home more and more, thereby reducing her contact with the townsfolk. She rarely saw women, children. When she did see them, she spoke kindly and they loved her as before. But she avoided them. She hoped to forget her need and hence squelch it.

She became a seamstress and gave her handicrafted pieces to a merchant in town, who sold them for her and shared in her profits. She looked at the money the merchant placed in her hand and had nothing, no one, to spend it on. She tucked it away. At first she sewed all sorts of things, dresses for moon-faced little girls, the softest babies' baptismal gowns. But she soon learned these things, mere things that had no white bones to snap, brought the taste of hate to her tongue. She turned instead to tablecloths. She embroidered better than anybody and gathered effusive praise, yet still the work gave little satisfaction.

She dug a garden, modest in size and output, which met most of her needs. She ate her homegrown meals late at night, for the dark made her food smooth. She did her best to go the path alotted to her in this life.

One day as she was carrying a large bundle of material home, a voice spoke to her. "You can have it. You know that."

She looked around, but only halfheartedly. There was an undeniable inevitability about this voice. She knew it came from within.

"All you have to do is want—want hard, want long, want enough. And it is yours. Everything is yours."

She whispered, "And in return?"

"Work for us."

But the woman didn't want everything. She wanted one thing, one dazzling chip off the diamond of life: a daughter. Her daughter. To love and hold. To cherish.

The cost was lowered accordingly, for even the devils have a sense of balance. She would be given a single gift, a way with plants. In return, when her daughter came of age, for surely with her gift she could find a way to get a daughter, she would explain to her the fundamental choice in life, and she would try to persuade her daughter, too, to join the side of the devils. Everything must be open, every detail made plain to her daughter. And her daughter, likewise, must be open completely in that moment, virginal and unencumbered, tied to no one but the woman herself. That was all. A simple bargain. No evil to practice. No blood to spill. Just one last hitch: Eternal damnation was hers.

The woman thought it over. With her decent, God-fearing upbringing, she kept expecting herself to be tormented. Good people were tormented by such dilemmas; this she knew. But she wasn't. She was almost without emotion. Her brain ruled her. She kept all senses on alert. She went to church and listened. She got on her knees and prayed. She knew she should talk to her priest. But her priest was a doltish sort, and she didn't like his crooked teeth and wandering eye. So she talked directly to the heavens, which met her entreaties with dense, white, silent clouds. Clouds you could climb the mountain peaks to, clouds you could stand in—and she did. But still they didn't speak. It seemed the side of good wasn't ready to vie for her.

If the answer didn't come from above, perhaps it would come from below, from immediately below her feet. She became fascinated with the dead. She went to every burial. She wandered in the cemetery. She put her ear to stone and dirt. She listened hard until she was quite quite sure: No voices spoke from death's doors.

And she knew she doubted. She doubted all that she had been raised to believe.

She realized she could not seek heaven's help, for doubt itself made such help inaccessible. Cold, still, clear, reasonable doubt now ruled her. She must decide, she knew, not on the basis of a sense of right and wrong, taught to her as part of a story of some Jesus whose lucky mother had him without trying, without even the benefit of a father. No. Instead, the choice must be made on the basis of a personal judgment: How much was a daughter worth?

Her emotions, which she had believed were as iced over as the mountain peaks she could see from her front door, the peaks whose clouds she had dared invade just the summer before, now answered, "Anything and everything." The answer was absolute.

Still, her brain kept working. She must think it through. What, indeed, was she giving up? If heaven did not exist, hell did not either, for one defined the other. And if she presented it all to her daughter, the whole matter of human life, and her daughter was free to make her own decision, what harm was there in that? She wasn't bargaining away her daughter's soul, only her own.

Which was bargaining away nothing. For without heaven and hell, what is a soul?

Her emotions and her brain were of one voice.

She agreed on a late March day, as the snow began to melt. That night she stored her needles and threads, her embroidery hoop, her linens and silks, in a wooden box. She went to bed and lay looking at the ceiling.

In the morning she was outside before dawn, picking at the half-frozen earth, but not in the area of her old garden. Oh, no. Now she knew just the right slope to plant a garden on, finding the most fertile soil exposed to the most sun rays without even knowing how she had gained the knowledge. She went to town and bought seeds of every type, even ones from other lands. It was a short walk to town, and the day was suddenly warmer. Farmers talked about perhaps planting early this year. The woman went home and planted that very day.

The peas sprouted first. Then the radishes, cabbage, cauliflower. Then the lettuce. So many kinds of lettuce. The woman's fingers now knew how to thin the seedlings as expertly as the farmers who sold their harvest in the market. She knew which would thrive best in which parts of the garden. Carrots, lima beans, potatoes. As things grew, she smiled in wonder. She interspersed flowers with the vegetables for added color. The asters came in silly profusion. The geraniums made a fine border. She never realized before how much she enjoyed flowers, perhaps because flowers were always on distant hillsides or in other people's gardens, never in hers. But now she let them bloom and she didn't feel frivolous—for the eye deserves its part, too. She planted vegetables from the south—zucchini and cucumbers, admiring their hairy stems and bright trumpet flowers. She planted vegetables from the New World—especially tomatoes, thinking ahead to the heat of August. People came from nearby towns to see her foreign eggplant and broccoli. Near the house the rhododendrons flourished. She wondered if this was evidence of her promised new gift or if this garden's abundance was the product of an early, unusually warm and sunny spring. But she didn't wonder much. Mainly she let herself rest in an inexplicable calm—a kind of contentment that she'd been denied since she had come of age. She didn't know if she was damned or not, but for now she was at peace. Eternity didn't matter.

The lettuces came ready for harvesting in May. Bushy and green and tasty. A neighbor woman had her eye on the lettuces, a pregnant woman. The barren woman knew that. She saw the pregnant woman peek out her window in the house that backed onto the garden. The pregnant woman asked to buy lettuce, the kind with the small, round leaves known as rapunzel. The barren woman said none of her vegetables were for sale. The pregnant woman peeked out the window day after day. Only the wall between the garden and that house kept the pregnant woman from entering uninvited and stealing the rapunzel. The wall was beginning to crumble in one spot. The barren woman didn't repair it.

One night the pregnant woman sent her beery husband on an errand of thievery. He climbed the wall and stole rapunzel. The barren woman watched him from the shadow of her home. She didn't stop him. She knew that in the house on the other side of the wall the pregnant woman was dining on her rapunzel. The pregnant woman was finding the stolen rapunzel more delicious than any other food she had tasted in her whole life, more delicious than any other food she could imagine. The barren woman closed her eyes and watched the pregnant woman eat.

That first time she saw with her eyes closed, she was frozen to the spot. When she opened her eyes at last, she sank to the floor, weak with awe. Was this her imagination or was this another gift—a gift the devils hadn't bothered to mention, it was so common among lost souls? For several days she didn't sleep. She allowed herself at most to blink. When finally she fell in bed, she was relieved to find just darkness behind her eyelids.

A week passed, and the pregnant woman craved rapunzel more each day. She nagged at her husband. And she was excellent at nagging, as well as loud at it. The barren woman heard and waited, her eyes open.

The man hesitated, though not from scruples. He did not understand why the barren woman would not sell the lettuce in the first place. If she was going to be so stubborn, she deserved to be robbed, for she clearly grew more than she could ever eat alone. No, the source of his hesitation was the fear of being caught. For thievery was not treated lightly. The man knew that well; he had stolen before and been caught before. Never again did he want to stand in the town square, locked into the stocks. He told his wife as much. The barren woman heard and waited.

Still his wife nagged. Her pregnancy was nearing its end. By early July the child would be here. If the man could steal a little rapunzel now and then just for another month, the cravings would end. And how likely was it he'd be caught on those few excursions into the forbidden garden? The woman with the garden was a reclusive sort. She probably went to bed early at night. She'd never catch him. And if the rapunzel was eaten quickly, there'd be no evidence of a theft anyway. The pregnant woman pleaded. The pregnant woman goaded. The pregnant woman ranted. The barren woman heard and knew the waiting was at an end.

Hours passed. The barren woman could bear it no longer. She closed her eyes and saw.

The man drank many beers. Then he climbed the wall in the moonlight and picked rapunzel.

The barren woman stood behind him when he got to his feet. "Thief."

The man held the rapunzel tight. His face in the glow of the moon said it all: The woman was alone, and as long as she didn't scream and no one else saw him in the garden, it was her word against his. His voice was testy: "It's just a few leaves. What do you care?"

The woman stepped back. She wasn't sure why. Her feet moved of their own accord. Yet she knew she wasn't giving up. Her senses told her that.

The man wasn't about to hesitate. But before his feet could move, he found his path blocked with waist-high thistles. He turned in a circle. The thistles were on all sides. They grew higher by the moment. "Help!" he called. "Help me."

The thistles stopped growing. They were now up to the man's chin. They pressed against his bare arms. He writhed from the sting. She knew he wanted nothing more than to jump from his own skin.

The barren woman watched, fascinated, breathless. "Take the rapunzel," she said when she could speak at last. "Take it with my best wishes. And in return give me one thing. One thing, and then ..." She paused, for she did not know the extent and limit of her powers. But she said what she hoped: "Then I will let you go home, your path clear and your hands filled with rapunzel."

"Name your price," hissed the man, hunching his shoulders together, trying his best to shrink away from the crowding thistles. "Anything!"

The barren woman saw the welts rise on his neck. She knew they were rising on his arms and legs. She was almost sorry for him. Almost, when she saw the revulsion in his eyes as he looked at her. She spoke coolly. "When your daughter is born, bring her to me. She will be mine."

The man blinked. The barren woman could see the effort in his eyes: He was trying to think of his round wife; he was trying to think of the child within her. He tried and tried, but the thistles stopped him. The thistles tortured him. And now they grew again. They ate at his cheeks. They would be at his eyes within seconds. "Yes!" he screamed. "The child is yours."

He went home, as the barren woman had promised, safely and loaded down with rapunzel.

The barren woman went home, as well, exhausted for no reason she could fathom, for surely she had done nothing strenuous. She sat on the floor of her bedroom and thought about what had happened in the garden. What she saw with her eyes closed was still a matter to be analyzed. But the thistles were not the result of an early spring, of an unusually warm spring. The thistles did the bidding of a separate force. The woman put her left hand to her mouth and bit a small chunk from the cushion at the base of her thumb. Cold water ran down her arm. The water of her veins.

Who would have thought it? Heaven and hell, the un-believable, were true. Divinity was true. She had bar-gained away much, after all.

But there would be an eternity to contemplate her choice. For now she should think of the immediate future. Of the child twisting in the woman's womb. Her own child. Dare she close her eyes and try to get to know the child? Not while the babe was in that other woman, no. The barren woman would wait till the child was free.

She slept outside that night, in her garden, near her rapunzel. Would the man keep his word? She remem-bered his eyes and thought he would. Still, she had to make sure.

In the morning the barren woman closed her eyes and

saw the man putting on his shoes, telling his wife he was going to the town square to warn everyone about the witch in the house on the other side of the wall, to rally them against her, to hang her or burn her, to rid the world of the scourge that was her. He walked to the door of his house and opened it to find grapevines, thick and gnarly, blocking the doorway. He closed the door and ran to the window. The room was suddenly plunged into darkness. Grapevines blocked every window. The man and his wife clung to each other in the dark. Finally, the man called out, "I will not mention the witch to anyone." And the vines receded.

Every hour on the hour the barren woman closed her eyes and saw the man wherever he was, the woman wherever she was. Once the man passed his priest and hesitated. When he opened his mouth to speak, the thistle poisons revived, and his body was suddenly covered again with welts. His tongue was thick with infection. He covered his mouth and ran.

Every hour on the hour the barren woman knew the child was hers.

When the child was born, a girl-child, as the barren woman had known she would be, this woman took her and traveled over mountain after mountain. She kept going until she could no longer hear the wail of the woman from whose loins she had taken the babe. Then she kept going until she could no longer remember that wail. The crying woman would have other children. Of course she would. She was a breeder; one look told you that. But for the running woman, the escaping woman, this child was unique.

She stopped at last on a small, high alm, several hours' walk from a town. A good place to raise the child, to savor her without the interruptions of others. On her first visit to town, the people eyed her coldly. A woman alone with a child was suspect, of course. Still, they were willing to take her money, that money she had saved from her seamstress days, in return for the land on the alm and a small home.

They became Zel and Mother.

I am Mother.

Zel brought all that I ever hoped for from love. I never intended to name her Rapunzel. I thought of Heidrun, Lore, Annelie. I thought of Brynhild, Gretel, Aurelia—even, in all their irony, Christa and Constance. Yet something within forced the name; something forced me to remember the source of the child. That same thing that forces me to come to town at intervals of no more than six months to touch an iron stone near the well in the marketplace and know its solid coldness. That same thing that turned my blood to water. But even that something couldn't stop me from shortening the name to Zel, a name that fit the child, for as she grew, she danced and leapt like the gazelles of Biblical stories, the gazelles I had heard much of in the church of my past.

When the babe was little, she nursed from my own breasts. I drank a brew my hands prepared from herbs my hands had picked, a brew no one had taught me. The milk flowed bluish and sweet, and Zel grew rosy and plump. I was in every way Mother.

Later I fed her lovely things from the garden, ever fresh and abundant. The girl smiled all the time. I rolled in the grasses with her, nibbling at her baby hands and feet; I splashed in the stream with her, tickling her girl tummy and underarms; I scrambled over rocks with her, pointing out the wild flowers—golden crepides, pink silenes, pale yellow saxifrages. And the girl laughed. We talked of the marvel of this world, and I taught Zel of her soul, the only soul I believed was available to us, the spirit of the here and now. Zel never asked for more.

Life was good. I ache with how good it was.

When I brought Zel to the tower that I had never heard of before but that my feet took me to all on their own, I did it to gain time. I needed to figure out how to lead Zel to the choice that would keep us together. I gave up salvation for all time—surely I deserved more than thirteen years in return.

I tried with the seduction of the goose. I remember word for word: "Zel, the gosling's eggshell has turned to dust." I leaned against the stone wall of the tower room.

"Poor little thing. I doomed it." Zel's eyes filled with anguish, for this was only five months after she'd entered the tower, and her face was still full of expression. Her face didn't lose expression until this past winter.

"If you had a gift for animals, you could have made the mother goose accept the egg."

"I'm good with animals, Mother. I tried my best."

"You're good with them, yes. But you could do much more."

Zel shook her head. "You mean like you said before? Talking to them? But even if I could have explained to the goose that the egg was for her to hatch and love, she might have rolled it away anyway. She might not have wanted another goose's egg."

I smiled. "But there's where the beauty of the gift is, Zel. If you had a gift for animals like my gift for plants, you could have made her take the egg."

"You can't mean a power that would let me force animals to do as I wished? Who would want such a power? I couldn't bear to be near an animal whose will I commanded." Zel's eyes showed a hint of the revulsion I had seen in the beery man's eyes thirteen years before.

I didn't speak. I reeled from the look in Zel's eyes. What had I done, after all? I hadn't really ever hurt anyone.

And now the wail of the woman rang out, the woman

whose arms flew over her head as her husband handed
Zel to me, the woman who fell to her knees and begged
me not to take the child, the woman who rent her clothes
in her grief. Would I never be rid of that memory?

Zel looked lost and confused for a moment, as though
my silence baffled her. "The gift of understanding and
being understood, now that would be a real gift." She
walked to a window and looked out. "Then I could make
friends here, animal friends."

Could I offer Zel that gift? My gift for plants was not
about understanding; it was about control. Would the
devils enter into that kind of bargain? Zel would have to
find out for herself. "Zel, remember when you and I
talked of God?"

Zel shook her head. She turned from the window and
looked at me with eyes of pure ignorance.

"The handyman's son said something to you about
'God willing' and you asked me who God was. Remember? And remember when we talked of praying?" I remembered it. I remembered my long explanation, how I
said some people, just some people, held these beliefs.
"You were almost six then; you must remember."

"I remember a little. But you'll have to tell me again. I
don't think about that boy much."

There was something about the way she said "that
boy," as though she thought instead about another boy.

Could she still be thinking about the youth at the smithy? She had to be tied to no one but me when I presented the choice. Me, no one but me.

I closed my eyes and I saw the youth and his horse, still searching for Zel. My Zel. My daughter.

I opened my eyes and considered Zel's face. In that moment I knew her thoughts encompassed more than me. I left.

Months went by. Seasons. At irregular intervals I would attempt again. But every time, I first tested Zel to see if the youth was still on her mind. And every time I kept my silence.

I had raised Zel wrong. I had raised a creative, curious child. I had let the child develop her own inclinations. I had clapped with pleasure at every new discovery, new talent. I had raised a child who could love easily and whom anyone could love back. Oh, what a terrible twist. I had raised a child in the best way I knew how, and it was that mistake that kept her from me now.

I hold that child in a tower. The only one I love, the one I love more than life itself; for two years I have held that one in a stone room.

And I live alone. I live the life I would have lived if I had never had Zel in the first place. Only it is far worse—for I know what I have lost.

Chapter 20 ❖ Konrad

onrad wakes tense. The carved wood that lines the walls and ceilings of the castle looks dense today, as though the humidity has made it swell. He lies on the feather bed with no cover, preferring to be open to the air in this hot summer weather.

Konrad tries to picture Zel. He doesn't trust his memory. Two years he searched for her. Two long years.

He was starting to think that he had perhaps imagined the girl. Perhaps the smith humored him, to pretend that there ever had been such a girl. Perhaps the toothless farmer was in on the conspiracy. Perhaps Konrad himself had participated in the hoax. For didn't his own mind conjure up a lone woman fiddler with a mindless goose that sat on a nest of rocks? There was no other explanation for the impossibility of finding the cottage on the alm.

And then this spring Konrad realized the much more likely possibility: His Rapunzel had married and left the canton. His Rapunzel could be anywhere. And she wasn't his Rapunzel.

The fiddle tune that infiltrated his dreams finally stopped.

That's when Konrad ceased to search and spent his days on nothing but work.

"The young duchess married more than a year ago," said Father one morning.

Konrad smelled his coffee, both hands circling the mug. He didn't look up. "This New World import gives us a great pleasure." He drank.

"I've heard of a young countess from the south with just the right character for you, Konrad."

Konrad's heart raced. He put down his mug. "Have you already made inquiries?"

"All the necessary ones. What do you want to know?"

If she was from the south, there was no doubt she would not have yellow hair. She would not braid it. If she was a countess, she would never be seen in smithies. If she was a countess, she would not give gifts to demented geese. This girl would be unlike Rapunzel. Looking at her would not hurt. He must ignore his racing heart. "Nothing," said Konrad.

"Good."

"A face-to-face meeting," said the countess. "We decided long ago that was the best idea."

Father scowled. "He's just agreed."

The countess shook her head. "I am as eager as you—more, even—for a suitable match. But we don't want another fiasco. He should meet the girl."

They both looked at Konrad.

If Konrad met the girl and his obsession for Zel made him decide against the match, the girl would be disgraced, and through no fault of her own. No, if they were to marry, they must simply marry. And Konrad must adjust and learn to love his wife. "Set the date for the wedding."

And so one month from now, Konrad will wed. His stomach knots at the thought. There is another life involved here, the life of an innocent girl from a distant land who puts her trust in Konrad. She wants to wake in the morning to a day that is full of pleasure and wonder. She wants to have children who make her laugh. She wants to love and be loved.

Konrad dresses quickly. He goes to the eating hall, where he finds his mother still seated at the table. Cut roses float in water-filled bowls. Their scent gives the air substance.

His mother smiles and nods, taking him in with one glance.

Konrad knows she doesn't approve of his simple clothing. As the wedding approaches, she seems to want him to look different—more suited to his position in life, perhaps. And his position has changed, for now he often attends meetings of the local legislature with Father. It has been agreed that he will stand in the next election. But

Konrad cannot apologize for his preferences. "I have no patience with fancy clothes." He sits at the table.

The countess pushes a plate of tarts toward him. "I didn't say anything about your dress."

Konrad scratches his neck. He's irritated at this talk, though he doesn't know why. "There are no formal events today."

His mother spreads her hands in explanation. "So you dressed for other work."

"Actually, I thought I'd take a day off work."

"Of course. You deserve it." She takes a sip from her cup and looks at him over the top of it. "You seem restless."

"I'm not."

The countess laughs. "You're argumentative today."

Konrad looks down. It's true. This is stupid bickering. He realizes he'd like to vent his worries about his upcoming marriage. Konrad speaks as if to himself. "You will have a daughter soon."

"And you, a wife."

Konrad wolfs down a third strawberry tart. It is early July, and since the spring he has eaten eggs with rapunzel for breakfast without fail. The passion for rapunzel is unrelenting. But today he will not ask Annette to cook him anything. He will not yield to the passion.

He stands. "I'm off." He leans and kisses his mother.

She takes his hand. "Are you going riding on Meta

today? You haven't been riding for months. Are you going today?"

"Perhaps."

"I thought you might. I woke knowing it." She nods. "And will you be scanning the mountainsides for homes you haven't seen yet?" Her grip tightens. "Konrad, my son, if you are to marry, you must give up past dreams."

His eyes meet hers. Agreeing to this marriage means he has not just taken a break from searching; he has given up forever. He stands tall and pulls his hand away. "I'm not looking through our mountainsides anymore," he says, wondering if his words are truth or lie, hoping they are truth. "I just need to ride."

The countess stands. "Yes. You could use a break from work."

That's what this will be—a break. "I'm riding out beyond the northern tip of the lake and over to the west side." No one lives on the west side. There are no doors to knock on. "The day promises to be sunny and clear."

His mother smiles. "Come home refreshed, for tomorrow we have your birthday festivities."

Konrad leaves the castle feeling more lighthearted than he can remember. He greets Franz with cheerful words. He brushes Meta himself, though she needs no extra currying. He mounts and rides out down the hill toward town.

A boy sits on a terrace, swinging his legs and playing

a fiddle. He plays a saint's song, so there is no danger. The music has nothing in common with the fiddle on the phantom alm.

The sun is bright on the lake. Swans have come in clusters. Konrad urges Meta up the mountainside to the west. This land is completely wild. There are no roads from here to town. It is good for the mind and the soul to be so free of human concerns. Meta trots in a southerly direction. Konrad expects nothing.

Chapter 21 ❖ Zel

The stone floor is warm. Zel lies with her eyes closed beside the hay mattress. A horse stands in the room and eats the hay. It stomps heavy hooves. Some mornings the room is filled with the goats she used to chase and milk, all of them eating hay. Zel laughs.

The horse chews and snorts, a wet, lumpy sound.

Zel shakes her head, harder and harder. She rolls from side to side. Each time her ears hit the floor they ring. Her chest rises in pain, her shoulder blades hold her up. Pain is lovely. It stands out from a vast sea of monotony. And now Zel sinks back, her head still. This horse is named Meta.

Meta swallows the last mouthful of hay. Now she will leave. She always leaves after she eats. Eats and leaves, eats and leaves, like the youth at the smithy.

But no. The chewing begins again. A tiny tug at her head. Another. Meta eats Zel's braids. The tugs get rough. Between tugs Zel has no respite, for her scalp aches. Her skin will rip. She wants it to.

The horse leaves. Zel knows she is gone by the lack of her smell.

Zel turns her hands palm down, runs her fingers across the floor. She finds the sharp stone. It took her twelve days to work that stone from the wall. Her fingernails broke. Her fingertips went raw. She opens her eyes and pushes the mattress aside. She scratches a line on the floor beside the other lines, each one marking a day. Zel pulls the mattress back in place. No one who enters the room sees the scratches. Zel laughs. No one enters the room.

Except Mother. Dear Mother.

Zel would take that sharp stone and dig trenches up the lengths of both arms. She would fill her room with blood. She would do many things.

But for Mother. Dear Mother.

Zel can't remember when it happened, but one day she ceased to ask about Mother's latest methods of fighting the unknown enemy. One day Zel realized she had no time for Mother's pitiful excuses.

But time is all Zel has, so much time. Like wild flowers, Zel has year after year. She used to paint the flowers' colors. Now she doesn't remember colors. She uses only charcoal. She draws herds and herds of stampeding horses on the walls.

She stands and walks to the wall. She shoves the stone into the crevice. Mother does not know about the stone. Zel hides it in the wall—as she hid her raw fingertips in her skirts when first she dug the stone from the wall. But she wears no skirts now. Zel laughs and spit flies from her mouth. It falls on her bare shoulder. She spits on her other shoulder. On one arm. On the other. On her breasts, her ribs, her stomach. And now she is out of spit.

She looks at her bucket of feces and urine against the rounded wall. Each month she leaks blood into that bucket. She takes the bucket and dumps it out the south window where the sun enters now. But she does not stand a second too long in the light. The sun's seduction has to be planned against. The sun tries to make her believe in colors.

Zel puts the bucket against the wall. Mother has told Zel not to dump her bucket out the window. She says she will empty the bucket into a hole she has dug. She speaks of cleanliness.

Zel keeps her dress clean for Mother's sake. She steps into it the moment she hears Mother calling. She steps out of it the moment Mother leaves. She is dressed, clean, and well behaved for Mother. All out of habit. She no longer thinks about why she obeys, why she walks or sits or talks or eats.

She cannot put that dress on and take it off over her head because of her hair. When she is not in her dress, she is naked. At least in late spring and summer. For other times of the year she has a thick cloak. It suffices, for the ivy that covers the tower holds in the heat of Zel's breath in winter. The coarse wool of the cloak rubs her skin raw. Sometimes she dances till her back bleeds from the rubbing.

Zel wears the dress one hour each day—Mother's Hour. Mother loves this highly embroidered dress that she gave Zel for her thirteenth birthday. The dress with the generous darts and hem that Mother let out ·as Zel grew. It is now full in the bodice. Mother says Zel looks beautiful in the dress. Beautiful to whom? Zel laughs. Her womanhood is wasted.

Mother has never noticed that nothing on the dress frays. Mother has never guessed that Zel goes naked. Mother doesn't know what Mother doesn't want to know.

Rascal chatters from the walnut tree. Zel races to the window. She crosses her arms on the high ledge. "Rascal, Rascal, tell me a story."

Rascal flicks his black-brown tail. In the winter he stands out shamelessly against the snow, but now he's one more variation in the shades of summer shadows. Zel rests her chin on her arms.

The squirrel jerks its head toward her.

"Wait, you little glutton." Zel laughs. She gets her breakfast roll and returns to the window. Zel no longer fashions tasty shapes. She tosses a dough ball.

Rascal catches it and eats.

This is their secret routine.

Zel and her sharp stone. Zel and her squirrel. Mother knows nothing of these pairs.

Zel unwraps today's fruit. Her fingers make indentations in the peach flesh, but only if she presses. It is of exactly the right ripeness. Not a single blemish. Mother takes such care.

Zel smashes the peach on the hot stone of the window ledge. She bites from the mutilated side. The juices run down her chin, her neck. They dry, pulling and tightening her skin in streaks. She bites again and waits again for the juices to dry. Again. And again. The smashed side of the peach is gone. Zel sets the remaining perfect half on the ledge.

The ants march in file to her offering.

It took weeks for Zel to lure ants to the top of her tower. She held her arm out as far as she could and squeezed a bunch of black grapes until the juices landed on what she hoped was the very bottom of the tower. The next day she squeezed a new fruit, but now she held her arm not quite so far out, so that the juices fell a little higher up the tower side. Each day she made the juices fall higher. She cursed the day when Mother brought a banana—strange tropical fruit, dry to the touch. But then she pureed the banana with spit between her fingers until it dripped easily. The plan worked because the tower's sides slope lightly outward.

Once Zel had a colony of lice. Her impeccable searching led to their discovery in the paper covering her boiled eggs. Mother must have set the freshly gathered eggs near the paper before she cooked them, for these lice were of the kind that live on hens. Zel kept the lice rolled up in plum skin. She fed them daily, a drop of blood from her tongue, which she would bite. She invited them onto her head. If they would only have taken up residence in her hair, she could have persuaded Mother to shave her head. But they preferred her tongue blood. She tried denying them blood altogether. They waited patiently. One day she dropped them into her crimson ink. Zel, who had once considered all life to be admired, wiped out the lice colony.

The ants eat the peach. Zel could throw the peach

with all her strength. Then she would be an ant killer, too.

Zel and the sharp stone. Zel and the squirrel. Zel and the ants.

And that's not all. Zel throws her head back and warbles deep in her throat, passionately like a pigeon in love.

Pigeon Pigeon flutters to the window. Her graceless body bounces heavily on stick legs; her eyes are stupid. Her gray belly matches the stone, but her head is white with brown speckles. A thoroughly unattractive creature. "I love your ugliness."

Pigeon Pigeon warbles.

"Ah, you've been sitting on the roof, have you? You heard the horse stomp inside my room. You swooned in the horsey air."

Pigeon Pigeon warbles.

"Oh, you were so excited you almost plummeted from the tower like a stone, you clumsy creature?" Zel steps back. "Are you trying to make me envious, talking of plummeting?"

And now Pigeon Pigeon is silent.

But Zel knows the bird will speak again soon. Pigeon Pigeon is a chatterbox. They used to argue over matters of import, like what the alm must look like on a May morning, or the smell of the cottage kitchen at dusk, or the thickness of Zel's rabbits' fur in winter. But Zel no longer listens to that sort of talk.

Pigeon Pigeon was the one who taught Zel to warble, to bob her head forward and backward. In turn, Zel taught Pigeon Pigeon to say, "Who? Who?" to the moon. Who is it that stalks Zel?

The moon is Zel's last friend. The moon listens to Zel and Pigeon Pigeon's questions, but she never answers. This is a deep kind of friendship, a union of cores.

Mother doesn't know about the moon. But she knows about Pigeon Pigeon, and she is repulsed by her droppings. Zel puts her finger in a fresh dropping now and draws a chalk-white pigeon head on the back of her hand. She does not yet think about how she will conceal this drawing from Mother. She is titillated at the danger of leaving the drawing on her hand.

Once Pigeon Pigeon built a nest on a window ledge. Mother swept the twigs away and rubbed spores of toxic mushrooms on the stones.

The mountain girl Zel was loves those windows. The mountain girl she was knows the world beyond the windows is not a dream.

Dreams are full of horses. And a youth.

Pigeon Pigeon coos.

Zel coos back.

Pigeon Pigeon never tried building a nest on any window ledge again. Zel took to cleaning up Pigeon Pigeon's droppings with bread crust. She throws them in her waste bucket. Friends can be intimate.

Like dreams.

Zel and the sharp stone, Zel and the squirrel, Zel and the ants, Zel and the pigeon. Zel and the moon.

Sometimes Zel hates them all. They come and go as they please. Even the moon seems to have ways to control her appearances, contriving special events with the clouds.

Zel thinks again about the youth with the horse. He had mixed feelings about her, feelings she saw in his eyes, feelings she often dwells on through the long hours. Their memory makes her warm when the whole world is frozen.

The youth has dark hair. Zel has light hair. The youth is rich. Zel has only her papers, quills, paints, brushes. The youth travels the world on a horse. Zel makes a world of a tower room. That they ever met was an accident. That she remembers him is but the result of her inexperience. She has no reason to picture the high curve of his eyebrows. She has no reason to yearn to put both hands on his face and let his eyesockets leave their imprint in her palms.

Zel looks at Pigeon Pigeon now with a fierce and sudden need. Fat Pigeon Pigeon can fly. But thin Zel cannot even move freely within the tower.

Zel's hair lies in braids coiled in the center of the floor. She walks around the room with just enough braid un-

coiled to allow her to stand at the windows. When
Mother comes, Zel lowers her braids out the window.
They reach clear to the bottom. Once they were long
enough to touch the ground, they stopped growing.
That's when Mother took to climbing Zel's braids to the
tower room.

Zel has asked Mother to cut her braids. After Mother
has climbed in, Zel's temples ache horribly. And, oh, after
Mother leaves, Zel's head pounds. Once she tried to gnaw
through her braids, but her jaw wouldn't do as she told it.
It snapped dryly at the air.

Mother says the braids are necessary. Zel has asked
her to use the walnut tree, like before. Mother doesn't
answer.

Zel walks now to the center of the room. She picks up
a braid. She looks at Pigeon Pigeon.

Pigeon Pigeon warbles. The bird walks up and down
the window ledge. She stops. She stretches a wing. A
wing!

Zel throws the braid as hard as she can. It slaps
Pigeon Pigeon from the window—*squawk*—it hits the
tree, catches briefly, then falls away loose, yanking hard
at Zel's temple, radiating pain through her head and
neck.

Zel shrieks. She has killed Pigeon Pigeon. Oh, cursèd
is the hand that tossed the braid. Zel kneels and smacks

her forehead on the stone floor till blood runs into her eyes.

Oh, she should fall to the ground like Pigeon Pigeon. She should be smashed and lifeless on the ground.

The ground. The ground beneath her feet, dusty in the summer, muddy in the spring and fall, frozen in the winter. Oh, to run in a straight line as far as she wants. To run so fast no enemy can catch her.

Sometimes Zel is sure that there is no enemy, that Mother is not right in the head, that Mother has imagined all. But when she has tried to question her, Mother's teeth chatter. She grows icy. Mother knows: Something out there is a mortal threat.

This day is starting badly. The morning is already slippery. Zel pulls her braid into the tower room again.

She is almost fifteen. She should be married, with child, baking bread and weaving cloth. She should not be alone.

Zel picks at the crusted juice on her neck. She goes to her bucket of rainwater and washes body and face. She looks at the drawing on the back of her hand. She washes it away roughly. She does not deserve to hold the memory of a friend she killed.

Zel goes to her stack of papers—a thick stack of fine linen paper, another sign of Mother's endless generosity—and lays one sheet on the floor. She paints

Mother weaving a hoop basket. Mother will like it. Mother is skilled at basketweaving. After all, those baskets are made of reeds, and Mother has a way with plants.

Zel takes another paper off the stack. She knows before she begins that Mother will not like this picture. She feels her blood heat. She paints their billy goat mounting a nanny. She paints in rapid, messy strokes. Her fury fills the page. She stands and runs her hands down her body. She digs her fingers in, leaves the whitest of marks on each thigh. She bends now and crumples the paper and dashes to the window and throws the paper.

It almost hits Rascal, who chatters at her in rage. Zel thinks of digging her sharp stone from the wall and throwing it at Rascal. She could rid herself of two more friends with one throw.

Zel takes another piece of paper. She folds it down the center. She bends back the edges. The paper points, like a bird diving with wings outstretched behind. She paints on feathers, with quick, light strokes. Zel stares at the painted bird. It is not pigeon or blackbird or lark. It looks more and more like a sparrow hawk. She paints sharp, predatory eyes, extra layers of overlapping feathers. She finds she hums now, and the finding makes her almost happy. She will let her linen-paper bird sail into the pines. She licks her finger, then holds it out the window. The wind comes from the west. From the south window, where she is now, the wind will carry the bird toward the marvelous lake of her childhood. She holds the bird out.

But no. She can do better. She puts the paper bird on the corner of the ledge, close to the inside so it cannot fall out. She stretches her arms and holds on to the outer lip of the ledge. She pulls herself up.

Zel takes her paper bird in hand and stands. She has climbed onto the ledge before, but never stood. She lifts her arms toward the skies. If a strong wind should come up, and strong winds do come up suddenly in these mountains even in summer, she would have no grip. She would plummet, like Pigeon Pigeon.

Yet she laughs now. She can see much farther than she ever dared to hope. And the sun helps today. The sun is not being evil, after all. Zel can see a great expanse of green lake. She can even see the peak beyond which she knows their alm lies. She can see the dark opening of the grotto that she passed on her way to market. She breathes so heavily, her chest rises and falls. It is hard to keep her feet from dancing.

She kisses the paper bird. "Be my soul." She leans as far out as she dares and waits. A wind comes. Oh, merciful nature. Zel lets her bird fly. Over the pines and away and . . .

Oh! Zel teeters and catches her balance. A man on horseback has come riding from the north. The paper bird swoops. The horse rears. The man jumps to the ground and picks up the paper bird. He looks Zel's way. He waves the bird. He shouts words that are blown back into his mouth. His horse is Meta.

Zel is spellbound. This vision is new and so real, it hurts. It moves. Horse and man disappear into the pines. Zel jumps into the tower room, her arms clasped across her chest. She hugs her own ribs in terror.

THE KISS

Chapter 22 ❖ **Konrad**

The linen-paper bird is painted intricately, beautifully, mysteriously. Konrad keeps his eyes on the equally mysterious tower as he weaves his way through the trees. Did he really see her? His heart pounds.

Meta stops and stamps under the empty tower window. "Hello. Hello up there!" Konrad controls his heart. There's no reason to be frantic. He calls again. "Hello!" He listens hard. He hears nothing. He sees no one. But a woman was there. He holds the paper bird over his head and shakes it. His hand trembles. His heart trembles. "I saw you. Please come to the window again!"

"Tell me what my hands do," comes a voice from within.

Konrad is at a loss. He is dizzy with hope, and now she makes a command he has no chance of satisfying, and all that hope shimmers in the heat as though it would evaporate. He turns the bird in the sun. "They paint paper. They fold birds. They make magic."

Silence. Then, "Tell me my name."

Konrad's mouth goes dry. He must speak, and if he is wrong, his dream is gone. Oh, God, let Konrad be right. "You are Zel. You are my Rapunzel."

"Aha!" The woman's head and shoulders appear over the window ledge. "No real man would know my name. You are no one. You disappoint."

It is Zel! O blessèd day. "Come down. Come out."

"Tease me, will you? Well, that doesn't hurt, for you are no one. If you'd been real, I might have jumped into your arms. Which would have been mad, since then we'd both die." She laughs. "You terrified me at first. But now you do nothing. Go on; move back so I can see you better, no-one man."

Konrad shakes his head in confusion. The girl shows the same inexplicable impudence she showed at the smithy two years ago. And now he grins. Thank God for that. He pulls down on the reins and Meta backs up. "I am Count Konrad."

Zel laughs. "A count. Never in my wildest dreams did I conjure up a count before. And on sweet Meta." She laughs again. "You are more fun than the other visions, after all. Please go on. Amaze me, O superb vision!"

Konrad suspects now that the girl is addled. And though he can see only her shoulders, he knows she is still naked. She was healthy in body and mind when he met her in the smithy. Something has happened. She is ill; she needs help. "Put on clothes," he shouts. "I'm coming up." He jumps off Meta and walks around the base of the tower. It is filthy. Who comes and throws filth on the base of his love's tower? He is now back to Meta, who grazes contentedly in the dandelions. How can he be back to Meta without having come across the door? He walks around the tower again, this time pushing the ivy aside, pressing against the stones, looking for those that might move. And here, at last, is the door. But it feels as much stone as the rest of the tower. It is immovable.

Konrad stands below Zel once more. "How do you get in and out?"

"If I could get out, I would not be here."

"What!" Konrad's breath comes in swells. "You are kept prisoner?" It's monstrous. "Who is your captor? I will fight him! I will imprison him two days for each day the scoundrel has kept you in this tower. And his prison will not be a lofty tower, but a dungeon, a hole, a grave!"

Zel stares down at Konrad and speaks excitedly. "How dare you say words I would never think! I am not Mother's prisoner. I am her charge. She protects me. Even in my most wretched moments of despair, I never think of putting her in a dungeon. You shame me, wretched vision."

Zel's head sticks out too far for Konrad's comfort. She shows signs of recklessness. And her talk of her mother makes him wary. He needs to know more, but he hesitates to ask her too much too fast, especially while she is up so high. "How did you get up there?"

"Ah, pretending to be dumb? You can't fool me. You remember everything I remember, since you are my vision—and I remember very well. I climbed the walnut tree."

There is only one walnut tree on this side of the tower, but it is clearly stunted. Konrad runs once more around the base of the tower, but there are no other walnut trees, only pines, and all have branches that come no closer to the windows.

"How long have you been up there?"

Zel shakes her head at the question. "Two years and three days. Tomorrow will be my fifteenth birthday. You know that. You know all and only what I know. You disappoint again. You bring me nothing new. But tomorrow Mother will bring me something new. Sheaves and sheaves of papers." She laughs so hard, she ends wheezing.

The girl has been in this tower for two years. While Konrad was wandering the mountainsides, she was pacing the stone floor. Even in his worst moments of loss and need, he had been a thousand times better off than Zel. He would tear the tower down stone by stone if he could. He quells the shout in his throat. He may need Zel's cooperation if he is to get to her, and, though she is half mad, she is bound to turn away from him if he shouts. "Mother comes tomorrow," says Konrad finally.

"Mother comes every day. You know that. Mother will be here within the hour."

Konrad speaks almost nonchalantly, not wanting to alert Zel to the import of his words. "Will she come up into the tower?"

"You know she will. Your pointless questions tire me." Zel rolls on the ledge. Now all Konrad can see is the back of her head.

"How does Mother come up?"

Zel disappears. "Go away, vision. Paper is better than you."

Konrad thinks of calling to her, then thinks better of it. This Zel is unpredictable. The tiny prickle of incipient horror makes his ears tingle. He cannot wipe away the image of a body falling from the tower window.

Responsibility makes Konrad instantly clearheaded. He rides Meta up the hillside till she is out of sight of the tower. He is almost certain Mother will come from the lakeside. He ties the mare to a tree, making sure she can graze easily. Then he breaks a lower branch off the pine and races back to the tower. He brushes away all prints of horse and man, walking backward into the scrub. He thinks of climbing a tree for a better view but remembers

Zel's fantastic claim that she and Mother climbed the walnut tree to enter the tower. He must not be near the walnut tree when Mother comes.

Konrad positions himself entirely within a scrub cedar. The bush scratches at him. He can see two sides of the tower. If only Mother comes to one of those two sides. He realizes that if he can see so well, then anyone who scrutinizes the scrub cedar may see him. He digs both hands into the dry earth and rubs dirt on his shirt and cheeks. His face is feverish.

Chapter 23 ❖ *Mother*

walk to the cabinet I have built for my fiddle. I play slow and fast. Soft and loud. As I play, my memory works past veils of pain and deception to thirteen years of happiness. The memory aches exquisitely.

I put the fiddle down. It is time to head for the tower.

I walk out, my cheek turned, so that I will not see the goose sitting on the seven silent lumps in her nest. Cursèd, faithful goose, who comes every year.

The day is hot. My blood warms like a turtle's. I want

to remember Zel as the effervescent child, but I cannot deny that that child is now withdrawn like a turtle. *Something must change.*

Sweat pours down my temples and neck, soaking the back of my dress as I lean into the slope of the mountainside.

At last I arrive. For the next hour I can simply be Mother.

My nose betrays me. It smells horse. But this is wild land. There can be no horse around here. Yet the odor is unmistakable. It is already noon, and Zel awaits me. I will investigate the odor later, when I descend.

I sing up, "Rapunzel, Rapunzel, let down your hair. Rapunzel, Rapunzel, let me climb your golden hair."

Zel's braids drop from the window. I climb quickly. Then I stand in the center of the room and coil the braids neatly. "My Zel." I open my arms.

Zel rushes to me, her face speaking elation. But once she is in my arms, her grip tightens. Dry sobs rack her body. I hold her at arm's length. "Zel, Zel, my baby. What is it?"

Zel shakes her head. She puts her hand over her mouth. She chokes on a dusty sob.

I won't have this misery. I slide the bag off my shoulder. "I've brought your favorite things." I hold forth an oval blue-black plum. "And there are grapes for your breakfast tomorrow."

Zel's hands are in constant motion, pressing on her cheeks and throat. "You brought no lettuce, no rapunzel."

I have not allowed my eyes to rest on that lettuce since the day I erred and said Zel had inherited the love for it, the day everything went wrong. "I can bring endive and chicory. Or southern lettuces: romaine and radicchio. Tomorrow, Zel. Whatever you like, tomorrow."

Zel takes the plum and throws it out the window.

I watch where the plum disappeared. Zel cannot mean her action. She needs the food I bring. She is grateful. I fumble in the bag and bring out a package. "Ham. Oh, my precious, my sweet. I gave a passing peddler a whole round of fresh cheese for his smoked ham because I know you love the taste."

Zel stares at my lips and brushes at her cheeks, as though she were really crying, though no tears come. She blinks continually.

I take encouragement from her intent eyes. I hold out a white bun. "I put a spoonful of sugar in the dough. It will be more delicious than ever. It will contrast with the salt of the ham. Tonight you'll have a special meal—for tomorrow, you know what tomorrow is."

Zel reaches out one hand and touches my lips. Her other hand wipes imaginary tears. She stares.

I brush her hand away. "Tomorrow is your birthday, Zel. I will bring you surprises. And, Zel," I say slowly, "if there's something you've been longing for, tell me. I'll do my best to bring it."

Zel still wipes at her dry cheeks. Her sobs are raucous. My daughter has never acted like this before. *Something must change.* Or maybe something has already changed. I am pulling at the skin on my neck. "Tell me, Zel, did something happen? Are you sick?"

Her eyes register sudden understanding. She nods her head vehemently. "I had another vision."

I nod, as well. "Goats?"

Zel shakes her head harder and faster. Her hands go to her temples. She screams in pain.

I grab her by the shoulders. "Stop that!" I slap.

Zel stops. No part of her moves.

My hand stings from the slap. In all her life, I have never slapped my child. I am numb with shock. I dare not feel.

Zel's eyes widen.

I must go on. I move my face very close to Zel's. "Did you see the horse vision?"

Zel nods.

"Your hair is crusted with blood at the forehead." I am breathless. "How did you hurt your head?"

Silence.

"Did you fall?"

"What a stupid question. People don't fall on their foreheads."

Her words sting equal to my slap. I am tired of these loathsome visions. I walk to the mattress and press my hands all over it. "See? It is whole. The horse is unreal. The vision eats nothing."

"What is unreal can eat."

"Don't be ridiculous. Tell that horse to go away." I reach down and grab hold of one corner of the mattress. I lift it and inspect beneath, making a great show of my actions. "See, the vision ate nothing!" There are scratches in the floor. "What's this?"

Zel looks over my shoulder. She laughs.

"What did you use to make those scratches?" I take her shoulders again. "You have something sharp. What? Where is it?" I shake her. "Tell me, foolish child. You aren't well. You mustn't have anything sharp. It is dangerous."

Zel flops in my hands. "My birthday," she says.

I stop shaking her. "Your birthday."

Zel steps to one side. She takes my bag with steady hands. She reaches in and throws the roll out the window. Then the ham. Then the grapes. She looks at her hand.

I have never been sadder. I grope at the air. She must let me feed her. At least I can feed her. That is a mother's job. "You will go hungry tonight, Zel. You will wake on your birthday hungry."

"You can make me happy, Mother. There is just one thing I want for my birthday."

My heart stops. I whisper, "What?"

"Freedom."

I turn my back. "First things first." I get on hands and knees. I search the floor. I feel the wall from the bottom edge to as high as I can reach. I am taller than Zel, so she couldn't have hidden it higher than my hands know. I move clockwise, feeling, feeling. Ah, yes, here is the loose stone. I hear Zel gasp behind me. My fingers dig. The stone comes into my hand. I turn and face Zel.

Zel opens her mouth. "A sharp stone, Rascal, the ants, the moon." The words come as if intoned. She smiles. "Oh, yes, and the lice, but they are dead, every one of them. Now you know all my secrets. It is your turn to give, Mother."

I will not listen. Zel's words are gibberish. She is walking the edge of sanity. I have to fight my arms. They want to cradle Zel. I wish her small again, simple and trusting. I throw the stone out the window.

"And there was Pigeon Pigeon." Zel's words come like arrows. I recoil instinctively. "But I killed her, Mother. I'm so sorry, but I did it." She lifts her chin. "Your turn to give, Mother."

I know about giving. If Zel chooses well, I can give much. "I offer the gift of talking with animals."

"You know I ache for this gift." Zel smiles dreamily. "But, like you said, first things first, Mother."

I feel off balance. Zel seems suddenly older, wiser, stronger. I understand what she has said: Freedom is a prerequisite. Only then will she talk about the gift. Can I risk giving her freedom first? "I'll be back on your birthday, Zel." I go to kiss my daughter.

Zel ducks.

A cry of anguish escapes my throat. My eyes film over. I must keep moving. I lower the braids out the window. The lack of the kiss burns my lips. I am descending so fast I lose my grip and fall the final few feet. I half walk, half run down the mountainside to the lake.

I slapped my daughter. *Something must change.*

Chapter 24 ❖ Zel

The pain in Zel's temples is horrendous. She sits on the hot stone floor in her dress. She will dirty the dress. She has coiled her heavy hair around herself. Her temples bang. Her head would explode, should explode. Mother is gone without a good-bye kiss. And it was Zel who turned her face away, stupid, lost Zel.

"Rapunzel, Rapunzel, let down your hair. Rapunzel, Rapunzel, let me climb your golden hair."

Zel almost swoons with ecstasy. Mother has returned. Mother has forgiven her. Mother may even be crying, for her voice is rough and broken. Oh, Mother. Mother will kiss Zel and Zel will kiss her back. She lowers her braids out the window and waits. Second chances are ecstasy.

Zel stands, astounded. The man in the window jumps to the floor with a noise as though he is real. His weight on her braids was real. She smells his sweat. She sees the hairs of his arms, the mixture of confusion and hope in his eyes. His shirt and face are covered with dirt. "Who are you, dirty man?"

The man wipes at the dirt on his face. "I told you already. Believe me."

"Count Konrad." Zel pulls her braids up into the room.

The man smiles. "The dress becomes you." He blinks and adds in haste, "Though you are better without it."

Zel's cheeks grow hot. "Dirt becomes you, Count."

The man laughs.

Zel likes his laugh. It is unique. She could not have made it up. Count Konrad is here. Her head spins. Her hands fly in and out; they cannot stay still. He is real, she is real, he is real, she is real. "How did you get here? I mean, I know you came on Meta. I know you climbed my hair. But how, really, how did you get here?"

"I've been looking for you for two years. Today I found you quite by chance."

"Why? Why would you look for me?"

"Why do you remember my horse's name?"

Zel's cheeks flame now. "I live here."

Konrad's eyes go to the charcoal drawings on the walls, the mattress on the floor, the waste bucket, the stack of papers with pens and brushes. His voice is iron: "Not for long."

Zel's eyes burn. It is all she can do to keep them open. "If I leave the tower, my enemy will kill me."

"What enemy?"

"I do not know. Mother knows."

"There is no enemy."

"How can you know?"

"I have to know. It has to be so."

Zel blinks now. Her eyes hurt less. "It doesn't matter anyway. I have already made my decision." She feels a stirring of some part of her she'd forgotten. "I'd rather be killed in an instant outside this tower than die slowly within it."

"You will not be killed. I will come back with a rope, and we will both climb down." Konrad speaks with assurance. Then he hesitates. Zel sees him swallow hard. "You will come with me?"

"I will come."

Konrad's face flushes. He steps forward. "Zel, oh, Rapunzel, you need time to reflect." He stops. He licks his lips. He speaks softly. "Time to recover." Zel can barely hear him now. "And in time, I hope"—Konrad's words come out so slowly—"I hope you will marry me."

Zel looks at her hands. They seem strangers, disassociated from her. Zel is a series of separate pieces matted together with spider web. She holds her hands out to this Count Konrad, palms up, slightly cupped. "What can you put in these hands?"

Konrad looks at them. "My love and devotion."

Love and devotion are wispy. They are the things her visions are made of. They paint pictures that have shape and shadow but no color. Zel waits.

Konrad speaks a little more loudly. "Dust of the earth and beams of the moon."

Zel's lips part. Some nights she is at one with the moon. Perhaps Konrad can see the moon part of her. So he is aware of shape and shadow and moonglow. But can he see the rest of her?

Konrad looks into Zel's eyes. He seems to swim there for a moment. Then he takes a deep breath and bows his head. He kisses Zel's palms with the heat and tenderness of mortality.

"Yes," breathes Zel. "Yes."

Chapter 25 ❖ Konrad

onrad is insatiable. His hands press along Zel's hairline and temples, around the shells of her ears. They follow the crest of her throat and circle the thin stalk of her neck, ever knowing. He undresses her with trembling insistence. His mouth finds her perfect. He believes he tastes the heady maturity of ripe plums; the bitter edge of small, round lettuce leaves; the sweetness of fresh milk. He believes he might die, he might burst like the constellation of Perseus in August—a shower of shooting stars—but for her call, her cry, the knowledge that she needs him as much as he needs her. The years of deprivation hone the afternoon, the evening, the night.

He lies beside her now. Beside his true love. She is a miracle; she is woman, yet so much of what she says is childlike. She is without guile. Konrad knows Zel has been gravely harmed. Her talk is disjointed; at times she raves. And her hair. No earthly force could make her hair grow so long in two years, in twenty years, in a lifetime. Zel has suffered under an evil power. Konrad knows as well, he knows with more conviction than he's ever known anything else in his life, that their love will restore her, their love will triumph over whatever wickedness the world holds.

He sleeps.

Chapter 26 ❖ *Mother*

he market in afternoon is less crowded than in morning. The fish vendor is gone, as is the cheese vendor. But the fruits and vegetables yet stand in half-depleted pyramids. I will buy Zel a fruit in every nuance of color. She will forget the slap. She will kiss me again.

I stand at a table. The vendor looks at me with narrow eyes.

I drop my head. This is the first time I've been to town in two years without a kerchief covering my hair and cheeks. Once I realized the man with the horse was in search of Zel, I knew I could go nowhere without covering my face. I couldn't risk being recognized for the woman who walked with the young girl in braids. I feel suddenly naked. Yet this fruit vendor couldn't possibly remember me from the days when I came with Zel. I will pay and be off. But no. I have brought no money. I never planned to come to the market. How stupid it all is. I can have whatever fruits I want just by willing the trees to bear them before my eyes on the way home.

I spin on my heel and walk to the fine shops that line the perimeter of the square. I hold my head high. I don't care if people recognize me. This is my last visit to town without Zel.

I walk into the milliner's. I select a straw hat. I gaze at it fixedly. The hat folds in on itself, twists and curls and ages. I leave the store and wait out back. I wait a long while. The milliner is a dunce. Eventually, though, he takes stock, for now he opens the door and tosses the ruined hat into the trash pile. I retrieve it and put it in my cloth bag.

I walk into the cobbler's. The shoes are made of leather. I cannot control parts of animal. But, yes, there's a wooden pair from the north country. I run my fingers lightly over the surfaces. The clogs dry and split. "Ahi," I say loudly. I suck at my finger. "This splinter goes clear to my bone."

The cobbler looks at me with swift suspicion. Then he sees the clogs. "Forgive me, madam. I'll use them for firewood."

"They caused me pain. Surely they should cook my dinner, not yours."

The cobbler seems chagrined. "Of course." He wraps

the clogs in paper and hands them to me. I put them in my cloth bag.

And now I enter the tailor's shop. The burghers' wives have their garments fashioned here. A linen gown covers a wooden torso. I am lucky: The form is fresh spruce. The dress is completely stitched together and needs only finishing touches on hem and cuffs. I blow on the dress.

"Yes, madam?" The seamstress stands beside me in a black dress decorated with gold-lace filigree—proof of her skills.

"I'd like a dress like this one, but, oh . . ." I point and look disgusted.

Spruce gum seeps through the linen. Sticky stains streak the gown.

The seamstress cannot seem to shut her mouth. She stares.

I look haughty. "I'll come back another day. And I'd throw out that torso if I were you."

"Indeed." The seamstress picks up the torso and sets it outside by the alley. She wipes her hands on her apron and comes back in, passing me as I leave.

I peel the gown from the torso.

Tonight I will order the straw of the hat to rejuvenate. I will order the wood of the clogs to mend. I will order the linen of the gown to rid itself of resin. Zel will have a new outfit.

And what will she do in her new outfit? She goes nowhere. The last time she had a new dress was when she entered the tower.

Something must change.

I am walking the road home. I stumble. Suddenly I remember the smell of horse, strong near the base of Zel's tower. But Zel hadn't seen a real horse. She spoke of a vision.

Can I close my eyes and see Zel now? This past winter, Zel asked if I ever sat in the cottage and closed my eyes to see her in the tower. When I answered yes, she made me promise never to do that again. Merely looking around the base of the tower, though, would not be breaking the promise. I close my eyes. My mind walks around the tower. Now in a bigger circle. No horse. Zel is safe. I open my eyes.

I arrive home. I eat. I sew. The starry night passes and still I sit. Moonlight assails my eyes. My back aches. The thimble is stuck, I jammed it down so hard. I lay down the needle and thread. I work the thimble free. It drops and rolls on the floor. I don't pick it up.

I pinch the skin on the back of my hand at the knuckle. It stays in a ridge. I hold my thumb to the moonlight. As I suspected: The little indented rings of the thimble stay clear on my skin. I am not resilient. I grow old. Time is short.

Oh, for the ability to cry! Dry sobs stick in my throat.

I am as dry as Zel has been all these years. My chest heaves. What did Zel say? She spoke a strange list—ants and lice, Rascal and the sharp stone. She said she killed Pigeon Pigeon and she spoke of the moon. Oh! It is I who reduced Zel to that raving girl. Zel walks the precipice with eyes half closed. All because of me.

And the wailing in my ears won't stop.

I pick up the fiddle to fight off the wails. But it turns on me—it screams like January winds, like a bereft mother.

I don my shoes. I will not waste energy calling up the water plants to help me cross the lake. I will need that energy later. I practically fly down the mountainside to the road. No one is about at this hour but owls and foxes. It is Zel's birthday. And, oh, I left behind the bag of presents, the perfect outfit. But Zel won't want it. I know that. In a burst of clarity, I know everything.

I circle around the north side of town, to the west, and then come back south, now on the opposite side of the lake. My shoulders fold inward. My skin puckers like drying fruit, like kissing lips.

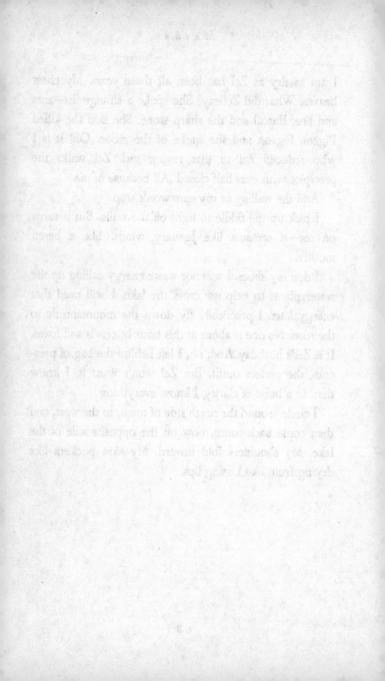

LOVE

Chapter 27 ❖ **Konrad**

erhaps it is the lack of moonlight, the stillness of the air, that wakes Konrad. He lies wide-eyed in the dark. Then the owl's screech comes, and he realizes there is a sliver of a moon, after all, enough to make out Zel's form beside him. She is lovely in sleep. Her breath comes in warm, gentle swells that make him absurdly happy. With one finger he runs a line down her forehead, down her nose, to her lips, which pucker now. Would that all his daughters should have such lips.

Zel opens her eyes as her head tilts toward his finger. "You are still here."

Konrad kisses her on the mouth. "Dawn comes soon. I have to leave."

"You are here now." She touches his left cheek, on his dimple.

"Of course I'm here now. But I must go." Konrad gets to his feet. "I'll return with a dagger and a rope." He thinks of the woman who comes every day at noon and climbs up his love's braids. He must be back well before noon. A dagger, a rope, an iron peg to attach the rope

to, a hammer to pound the peg in. He is now all business. He dresses quickly. The eastern sky lightens almost
imperceptibly.

Zel sits. "Stay till the sun comes." Her voice is the
murmur of deer nuzzling clover. It touches barely, leaving
the grass in wonder. "All I can say to the moon is 'Who?'
Do not be a man who goes with the moon."

Konrad flies to her side and hugs her. He should not
have let himself get so caught up in the job at hand.
There is plenty of time to ride to the castle and be back
before noon. Zel needs his reassurance. He has heard
enough, guessed enough, to understand why. "Believe in
me. I am. Just as you are."

They lie in silence, kissing. These kisses are at once
less urgent and more forceful than yesterday's. And this
passion so far exceeds that of his youthful dreams and
fantasies, Konrad knows: He would willingly give his life
for Zel. He gets up at last and dresses once more. He
walks to the window.

Zel follows without a word. She lowers her braids over
the ledge.

Konrad climbs to the ground. He goes uphill to where
he has left Meta this whole night. He does not look back,
though he knows Zel wants him to. He cannot, for fear
that he won't leave.

Konrad approaches the tree where he tied the mare.
This is where she should be. But the tree itself is gone

and the horse is nowhere around. Her reins, bridle, and bit lie on the ground. Konrad looks around in alarm.

He peers at the trees, every muscle tense. The horror returns—that horror he felt in the scrub cedar when he first saw Zel's braids fly from the window and watched Mother climb. He expects something, anything, a sign of watchful eyes, eyes responsible for the fate of Meta. "Advance," he says aloud.

No one attacks.

Instead, he hears the familiar whinny. He takes the reins and bridle and rushes through the brush and trees to a small meadow. Meta grazes. She turns a placid eye to him. Her smell, the ripple of her withers, they are like always. Her mane is tangled, but then, she has been all night on her own. She gives no indication of being enchanted. Konrad weighs the risk; he takes it. The bit and bridle slide on.

He rides with Zel's words in his mouth: "Don't disappear." His blood runs wild. This is what love is. This is what life is.

Chapter 28 ❦ Zel

el watched Konrad dress. She remembers the lock of hair that swings over his eye when he lowers his head, the glint of the belt buckle, the white flecks in his nails. Her mind draws him now. Her heart feels him. Her tongue tastes him.

She stares at where Konrad disappeared into the brush. She thinks she called after him, "Don't disappear." She thinks her call was loud. But she does not know. She thinks he was here, but she does not know. One moment can reverse the next. Life is slippery. Zel looks up: No stars are left in the sky. She turns around: No words are left in the room. She gulps the air. She would burst.

But she mustn't. All is near. She closes her mouth and forces the air through her nose. Her eyes can see the room and what fills it. *Believe the eyes. Believe the man.*

She makes no noise. If she violates the air with words, she will dissolve, like salt in water.

Zel touches the stain on the sheet, her wedding sheet, for last night she and Konrad vowed to love each other till death do them part. Konrad spoke in crystal tones. He said he would love her beyond death. And when she asked what that might mean, he looked at her in silence.

Then he said they'd have much to tell each other in the years ahead.

Zel pushes the mattress to one side and looks at the scratches in the floor. She cannot add one this morning. The sharp stone that had been her only night friend is lost in the woods. Zel traces the marks with her fingers. She would like to add one final mark as part of saying good-bye. Konrad is going to bring back a dagger. She can scratch the floor with the blade.

But what will Konrad do with his dagger?

Zel thinks suddenly of Pigeon Pigeon. When she climbs down, she will search, for Pigeon Pigeon deserves a proper burial.

Zel sits. A coldness enters her bones. Life is slippery. She mustn't stand or she'll fall. She has been happier this night than she has dared to hope for in these past two years.

But life is slippery.

She stretches out on the mattress. She turns her face to the window and gazes at the deepest blue of the sky. Her job now is one she's been well prepared for: She waits.

"Rapunzel, Rapunzel, let down your hair. Rapunzel, Rapunzel, let me climb your golden hair."

Zel stirs from the semiconscious state she knows how to ease into and out of at will. She rises from the mattress. She feels she walks on a cushion of air. Mother is here, but it cannot be noon yet. Mother is here and Konrad has not returned. Zel does not allow herself the indulgence of fear. Konrad has asked her to believe in him.

Zel lowers her braids from the window. She flinches as Mother climbs. It is hard to keep the nausea from rising. Zel puts both hands over her mouth to hold in the cry. Mother will never climb up these braids again, for she can exit the tower with Konrad and Zel, by rope. Endings exist after all. An ending, this. An ending to what seemed endless only yesterday.

Mother comes through the window and stands on the floor. She coils Zel's braids. Her face speaks shock and grief. "Do you always sleep naked?"

"Yes." Zel does not say that she dresses only for Mother's Hour. And Mother does not ask. It is clear to both that Mother understands Zel has kept secrets. They will not speak of this. A thin coating of kindness covers them—the result of yesterday's slap. They will not cause more pain than they must. Zel is grateful.

"The moon was crescent. The trollblooms are out." Mother speaks rapidly. "I surprised a small brown bear, lolling in the day lilies by a stream."

Zel cannot understand why Mother is speaking like this. Mother never tells of what she sees on her way to the tower.

"Did you happen to spy a rogue goat or a buck with wide antlers?" Mother grasps Zel's wrist tight. "Did you?"

"No, Mother."

"My mind plays tricks. I thought I heard hoofbeats when I was down near the lake. And yesterday I thought I smelled horse." Mother shakes her head with sudden deliberation. "Little is served by banter, Zel. We must speak. I have something to tell you."

"And I have something to tell you, Mother."

Surprise fills Mother's face. "What could you have to tell?"

"I'm leaving the tower, Mother."

Mother sways. Zel reaches to steady her, but Mother steps back and puts a hand against the wall. "We must talk of Heaven and Hell."

Zel is slightly alarmed by the randomness of Mother's words. But she won't be distracted from what she must say. She speaks with tenderness. "I don't have to stay here any longer, Mother."

Mother's back rests against the wall now. Her eyes seem to glaze over. "You have to choose, Zel. If you stay with me . . ."

"I will not stay in the tower." There is no animus in Zel's voice, only quiet mountain stones, the stones that make up a child raised on the alm. Her eyes are the fertile soil of Mother's garden. She knows both steamy earth and frozen rock. *Please, Mother, please see me. Please hear me. Please know me.*

"Of course, you're right." Mother nods quickly. "You can return to the alm. You can bargain for your gift there."

Zel hears the words, but she has trouble decoding them. Mother is rambling about a bargain. Zel must enter Mother's words and bring her slowly around to Zel's words. It is difficult for Mother. Zel knows how difficult, for, after all, was not she unbelieving when Konrad first entered her tower room? "I don't want to bargain, Mother."

"Of course you want to bargain. That's how you get your gift."

"What gift?"

"The gift of talking with animals."

Talking with animals. Yesterday when Mother promised that gift, Zel's heart lurched. Now it pounds. The gift is a natural one for Zel. "Give me the gift, Mother."

"First I have things to tell you."

Zel nods. "Hurry."

"We must do nothing quickly. Nothing thoughtlessly." Mother looks into Zel's eyes. As she talks, she seems to sink down the wall. "The eye of God is cool and graceful. But the gift can be as passionate and searing and twisting as you want. The depths compel exquisitely. They pierce to the core."

The words would wrap Zel in unfathomable silky threads, they would render Zel helpless to Mother's wisdom, but for last night. Zel has her own understanding, an understanding that allows her to find sense in Mother's words. "Dear Mother, I've known passion. And I will never give it up."

Mother is now on the floor. She looks up at Zel with hope in her eyes. "Oh, yes, I knew you would choose me. No mother and child have loved more passionately. But I must tell you certain things first. They won't matter, but I must speak. Then you can choose to live with me on the alm like before."

Zel shakes her head. Mother makes no sense, after all. She persists in confusion. Zel is sorry for her, sorry for a woman who cannot distinguish between the passion of mother and child and the passion of lovers. Is that why Zel's father left? "It cannot be as before, dear Mother." She reaches down and rests her hand on Mother's hair. The sun shines bright. "You are darker," she says, thinking of Konrad.

"Everything will out, Zel." Mother holds on to Zel's hand. "Your mother loved rapunzel."

Zel laughs at the craziness of this conversation, though

it could as easily make her cry. So Mother did love rapunzel, after all. She touches Mother's wide, raised cheek. "You are plumper," she says, thinking of Konrad.

"I . . . I made a trade with her. She took my rapunzel. I took hers."

Zel knits her brows. She is used to meaningless words In the past year Mother's voice has often not made sense. But usually that's because Zel can't make herself listen to the words. Today Zel fixes those words with a steady eye, yet still they make no sense. And, worse, there is something terribly wrong. She bends and holds Mother tight, as though her body could tell Mother of the joyous change and make Mother understand, make Mother stop saying things that would disturb despite their obvious perversity. She lifts Mother to her feet. "You are heavier," she says, thinking of Konrad.

"We had a lovely life together." Mother's hands run down Zel's back, tapping the vertebrae, playing the ribs. "Remember those years, Zel. All I had to give was my soul, and in return I got the gift that led to you."

Zel eases a little away from Mother. "Your soul?"

"A small thing in comparison with all that love."

Zel sifts through the words. So much is babble. But the part about Mother's soul she plucks out to pick apart. Mother always told her that her soul was that spirit with which she feels the glory of the world. Mother has traded her soul for love? How can that be? Souls and love shouldn't be balanced against one another, for aren't they made of the same stuff? Zel stares at Mother.

"Good, good. Keep concentrating." Mother smiles. "Zel, you are here in the tower because you have to choose. You can keep your soul and risk damning it some other way, perhaps never knowing love again anyway— for most people live loveless lives—or you can trade your tiny soul for a gift that can lead wherever you want."

Zel seizes on Mother's first words. "But the enemy?"

"What enemy?"

"The enemy." Zel's ears fill with the thunder of blood, heating, racing. Her lips curl away from her teeth. A hiss of pain escapes her. "You said I was in this tower because of the enemy who wanted to kill me. But now you say I am here because I have to choose.' Her voice rises. "Which is right?"

Mother raises a hand in front of her face. "They both are."

"No, Mother." Anger tempers Zel's voice. It is now hard as a dagger blade. "Which is right?"

Mother cowers. "It was a way of speaking. You didn't understand yet. I knew you'd make the wrong choice. So I called the wrong choice your enemy. It was just a way of speaking."

"You locked me in this tower; you made me think

someone wanted to kill me; you kept me from the plea-
sures of the world, from all company but one hour a day
with you, just because you thought I'd make the wrong
choice? What choice are you talking about, Mother?" Zel
is screaming now. "What in the world are you talking
about?"

"I'm not talking of this world. I'm talking of the
next." Mother huddles against Zel's shoulder. "Don't yell
at me, Daughter. Please."

And now Zel goes over all those words. "Daughter?
Am I really your daughter?"

Mother trembles. She curls in upon herself.

"Tell me! Tell me what you meant in those words before! Did you get me in a trade for rapunzel, for a handful of leaves? Did you really?" Tears weigh inside Zel's
lower eyelids. She has not cried for two years—all for
Mother's sake. She protected Mother from full knowl
edge of her sadness. The irony hurts. "Do not lie to me
ever again." She steps away so a full block of the stone
floor separates her from Mother, this woman for whom
she has no name but Mother, a lie in the very name.
And now Zel remembers Konrad's words when first he
appeared at her tower: You are kept prisoner. Yes,
Mother has imprisoned Zel. Mother has betrayed Zel's
love.

Mother totters and falls. "We have a bond of passion
no one and nothing can break. You have chosen me." She

puts her face to Zel's feet. "Cry for me, Zel. Feel my pain. Cry!"

Zel shakes her head. Her tears blur her vision, but they do not fall. Her rage already subsides. She is still alive after the knowledge of the indecent trade; the wound that cleft has not killed. The woman on the floor is no stranger; this woman has been family to Zel for as long as she can remember. And Konrad is her husband now. So Zel has everything she could want. Her happiness prevails. It heals fast and deep. And this woman's sadness prostrates her. Zel's voice softens again. "When I spoke of passion, I spoke not of you."

Mother looks from Zel's feet to her face. She closes her eyes. When she opens them, her voice comes raspy. "What is his name?"

Zel touches the top of Mother's head with the very tips of her fingers. This woman raised her. This woman was as good as a mother could be, until she thought Zel would leave her.

"His name. Tell me his name."

"Count Konrad." Both Zel's hands are now on Mother's head. They run down to cup her cheeks. What better reason for betrayal than this?

"Pity disgusts me." Mother slaps away Zel's hands. "I am the one who loves you. Me!" She grabs Zel's braids and pulls her down. She clamps her teeth and rips.

Zel shakes her head as the hair comes away. She is so

light, so light-headed. She could fly. No, she could float. She is dizzy. One moment reverses the last. What next?

Mother whimpers now. Her fists press tight to her own ears.

Zel is frightened for Mother. Her hands open instinctively. That's when she hears the noise. It is whisperlike at first, then windy, then like a tempest, as the branches stretch and grow. Those branches that Zel once wished would reach to her are now, at last, reaching into the tower room and twisting around Zel's waist. She cannot break free. Zel's scream is barely heard above the grind of wood on wood. Even within Zel's head the scream is almost lost.

Grabbed and stolen and flying.

SCATTERING

stand and watch Zel whipping from branch to branch, from tree to tree, the forest taking and yielding like hands passing a lit candle, until the girl is gone from sight and silence returns to the wood.

I fall back onto the mattress, exhausted. I am barely conscious. Only slowly do I realize what has just taken place. Zel is gone. Forever gone. How can it be? Twice defiled.

If only she had let her tears fall.

When Zel still stood before me, I closed my eyes. I saw within her womb to the cells that split and multiplied, to the act of God that punished me worse than anything else. Zel had it without a price. She had what I longed for. Women everywhere have it so easily and now Zel joined them, joined the legion of women who have what I never could. *Oh, God, what savage trick you played, to pick for barrenness a woman who couldn't bear to exist without a child.* Too much unfairness. Too much brutality.

That's when I heard green wood rubbing on green wood.

I am powerless against myself. I know the hideous.

"Rapunzel, oh, my Rapunzel, let down your hair. Rapunzel, Rapunzel, let me climb your golden hair."

The man sings in the same tune I use, the tune I have played on my fiddle so many times. I hadn't even heard the hoofbeats. But I knew he would come. I stand. My hands take hold of the ends of Zel's braids, ends ripped ragged by my iron teeth. I toss the other ends from the window. I feel the braids plummet, like dead birds.

The man's weight is less than mine. Just as Zel said, I am heavier.

His head appears, one leg climbing above his shoulder level, spiderlike. He sees me and stops, frozen. He blocks the sun; his face is lost in shadow. Nevertheless, I can see his skin is fair. Just as Zel said, I am darker.

"Count Konrad. You failed to kill the goose." I consider the rope coiled over his shoulder.

He works his way onto the window ledge. His eyes search the room. His shoulders jerk spasmodically. He crouches. He is thin. Just as Zel said, I am plumper.

Still, I am amazed I found the strength to hold on to those braids while this man climbed. First the trees stole my energy. Now this count used up more. Hardly any remains, and what there is can barely sustain the life within me. I pant in the heat. I still hold to the braids, more to keep myself standing than anything else. My mouth speaks with words that come from nowhere: "Life is slippery."

Konrad wipes the sweat from his lip. He pants as well. "Where's Zel?"

I consider the dagger swinging in his pouch. "I'll never see her again." I want to lean against the wall. I want to become the wall.

Panic plays in his eyes. His voice comes tremulous. "Where is she?"

I look at this ridiculous man, with the peg and hammer tucked in his belt. He thought he could steal her away so easily. He knows nothing, understands nothing. He will live his simple life and die his simple death. And he'll never know what ruin he brought to Mother and Zel in his clumsy stumbling into our lives. "You'll never see her again, either."

Konrad thrusts his neck forward, though he remains in a crouch. His eyes go to Zel's dress on the floor. He scans the mattress, the walls. Finally, he looks at me once more. And now I see his face well. His eyes. His mouth. He holds more misery than I realized a man could feel. And instantly I know what I never wanted to know, what I hate knowing: He is my soulmate—he loves my Zel. No! What have I done? The world is wrong.

Konrad's head falls back as the scream empties his

lungs. When there is no more left, he draws the dagger. "I will find her. I cannot bear the pain of living without Rapunzel."

"Nor can I," I whisper, each word costing more energy than I can afford, "but such is our fate. All is inevitable."

Konrad's eyes flame. He begins his lunge.

My fingers open as my hands rise in a move of self-protection. The braids fly. In that split second, from nowhere comes the image of Pigeon Pigeon being smacked from the window. From nowhere comes her squawk. And I know what will happen. I would grab the braids back, but they are already gone.

The braids whip Konrad from the window. Gone like the bird. Gone like Rapunzel.

No! I close my eyes and squeeze my hands together and use the final reserve of my strength.

Konrad is caught and pierced by the brambles that have sprung up around the base of the tower.

He lives.

I die.

Chapter 30 ❖ Zel

Walnuts. And pines. They carry her. And oaks, aspens and birches, chestnuts, larches, and now cedars and cypresses. Hour after hour, tree to tree, around lakes, across rivers, over mountains. She thinks nothing. She sees a sharp peak like a giant cat's tooth. She is in the branchy hands of a colossal sycamore, the skeleton hands of stubby olive trees. The cows change from brown with white faces to all white. Day after day, tree to tree. No tree hurts her, but no tree releases her.

And now she thinks. She knows. This is a careful conspiracy of leaves and branches. Night and day. And then darkness.

GATHERING

Chapter 31 ❖ *All*

A young woman stands on earth of many colors. People come from far away to see the range of those colors, from deepest ochre to palest cream. The woman paints on paper, inspired by the colors of the earth.

She doesn't always paint. She often uses that earth to fashion pots and dishes, vases and cups. Everyone who has the money buys her pottery, and those who can't afford to buy receive gifts.

She lives in a small home attached to other homes on both sides and below. She has become accustomed to the stone walls of this home, cold like the stone of the tower, so unlike the warm wood of her alm home. She no longer shrinks away when she touches those stones.

She loves the closeness of town. She talks to everyone who passes beneath her window, and today she talks to the travelers on the road as she paints the meeting of the sky with this land.

This land differs from her homeland—from the Alps of her past—in ways that turn her heart. She stops for a moment and lets her eyes follow the road till it twists out of sight through hills that tumble down to the sea. This is salt sea, whitish water, not sweet lake water. But, though she loves the sight of the sea, especially when it's turbulent, she has gone there only twice. She doesn't stray often from town. Fear can still seize her.

Three years ago the trees handed her over to a vine that stretched and stretched and deposited her in mounds of sand. The vine retreated. She slept.

When she woke, she saw only the glare of sun on sand. The air seemed calm. She refused to be fooled. Would they reach out for her again? Was this a way station or a final resting spot? She would not wait to find out.

She stood and called. Her voice fell dull on an empty world. Though she was bruised in all parts, hungry and dry and naked, she walked. With every step, gratitude filled her heart. Sand beneath her feet was a thousand times better than the stone of the tower. Freedom, even lost and alone, was superb.

When she closed her eyes, loss and fear and, finally, rage burned red inside her head. So she worked to keep her eyes open. She blinked only when they were so dry she screamed from pain.

Night followed day followed night, and she lost track of time. But her feet wouldn't stop. There were no curved walls to limit her path. She could go as far as she dared.

And then her energy was spent.

She opened her eyes finally to water trickling across her cheeks. People stared at her, speaking in a nonsense tongue. The crickets screamed in midday, "Desert, desert, desert." She looked around and saw the town hugging the hill. The insects were crazy—for this was no desert. She had walked to a far better land. She gaped at pink and red and white oleanders, blue hydrangeas, yellow mimosa, violet bougainvillea. She shook her head with wonder at the palm trees and yucca, things whose names she had yet to learn.

The wind, a dandelion seed on a summer day, whispered, "Banishment." That tiny wind was as foolish as the crickets. Banishment to these colors could have been a blessing in disguise for an artist, if the taste of water at last hadn't brought the longing. She trembled at how quickly the longing came and settled within, at how quickly her mind absorbed what had happened and didn't close up at the horror but took it all in and in and in, then stayed open to welcome the longing for him.

She sat on the dirt, wordless. They lifted her, half-starved, dry as a bone. They wrapped her blistered body, her burned feet, in cloth soaked with oil. They fed her juices of miracle fruits. And she thought to go in search of him immediately. But when she got up from bed, she retched. When she ate, she retched. A sudden movement, a particular smell, could bring the heaves. She realized she couldn't travel until she recovered.

The women accepted her like the earth opening itself to rain. They laughed and caressed her. Yet the young woman kept retching even after the blisters had healed. The women nodded knowingly. They fed her bread. They taught her a new tongue, brought her to church. And by the time the retching ended, she saw her own gently rounding belly and realized she would have to delay her searchings, for other matters pressed.

The woman listened to those around her. Slowly her gratitude turned into friendship. She makes all their care fruitful in every way she can. She helps in the garden, painting the fences and trellises so the blue and pink clematis vines can twine in abandon. She helps in the house, carving pot plugs from the bark of the cork oaks that color the air with their silver green leaves. She helps in the barns, her soothing ways yielding more milk from one sitting than the other maids get in three.

The people have grown to love her. They respect her devotion and slide over easily to make room for her in the church pews. The family that took her in lives downstairs from her now, for when the twins were born, she needed a place of her own.

When they first told her she should move to the rooms upstairs, fear flickered in her chest. She insisted they build two more sets of stairs, one in the rear straight out to the garden and one in the front straight out to the street. And even now every day she races up and down all three staircases several times. She comes and goes as she pleases.

She grows a tangy lettuce with round leaves and gives it to anyone who wants it. People laugh teasingly at this strange, small gift. Her answer is another handful of leaves. She prays that no one anywhere will do the rash for want of rapunzel.

And there are other things she does that they call peculiar. She holds tears in her eyes, even when she smiles, even when she laughs, but she never sheds them. She wears no ring, but she talks of her husband, for whom she will go searching as soon as the twins are old enough to travel. And she does not touch live trees, though lately she has consented to sit with others under a fig.

She has many ordinary ways, though. She eats at normal hours, sleeps at normal hours. She never speaks out of place. She bows her head when she should. But sometimes, still, she finds herself counting feathers in the milliner's, cheese wheels in the milk shop, baguettes at the baker's. And she realizes she lost herself for a moment. That's when she reminds herself that life is no longer slippery. The urges she felt to self-destruct ended when the torture ended. The madness stayed in that tower. She is here.

Is she safe?

She doesn't believe in safety. She believes in life, in all its beauty and fragility. She has her daughters. She has her art. She feels rich. Her soul mends.

The woodpecker that pecks now is in a parasol pine. The air thickens with the smell of rosemary shrubs. Sunflowers peek over a wall at the edge of town. This land could not be more alien. Even Mother would feel assaulted by the profusion of plants. But this is home to Eve and Hélène, the two-year-old twins who now collect stones tossed here by the mistral wind that blew all day yesterday, that cried like ghosts.

"Time to go home, girls."

Eve and Hélène, both naked and brown, have nowhere to hold the stones so carefully selected. The woman offers her skirt, and they load it up, all three counting together. Ten stones, the size of fists. The woman knows somehow that this number is right for the stones, though she cannot figure out where this feeling comes from.

At home the girls sit out back and poke fingers in paint. They decorate the stones with dots, lines, handprints. The woman is overcome with the ferocity of her love for these children. She pictures two women standing in a doorway bargaining—the first hands over lettuce; the second hands over a child. She knows this is not the real picture. She will never know the real picture. But in some way, this has to be the right picture. She has lived need. And one in need can do the dreadful, the unthinkable—trade lettuce for a child, lock a child in a tower.

These precious children push the stones together, nestle one against the other, like eggs in a nest. Ten. The woman looks and remembers finally. Each year the goose added one more. It was five the last time the woman saw. It would be ten now. The woman scans the sky for a stray goose. Then she shivers and puts the girls to bed.

The woman stands at the window and contemplates what sleep might bring. Her dreams hold on to almost thirteen years, good years. Mother was a good mother. The alm was a good place to stretch and grow. Her nightmares hold on to two years of granite that won't respond to her touch, wildlife that doesn't come to her call, a waste bucket and a mattress and a stack of papers and paints and brushes and a sharp stone. And, finally, trees, branches, leaves, for hours and days. Mother was a witch.

The woman has read and reread the faces of the people of her town. They are good faces, kind faces. She looks into these faces and she believes there isn't a one of them who wouldn't sell his soul for the right price. She has to believe this. She loved Mother. When she murmurs tender words in her daughters' ears, when she caresses them and combs their hair—hair she never plaits, will never plait—when she bakes them the dark breads of her childhood, she touches them with the flesh of human charity. Her heart opens. Even to the woman who traded away her child, the unknown woman, whom this young woman works to keep herself from searching for in the face of every older woman who passes.

This young woman owes her life to the unknown woman. She owes her soul to the witch woman.

But lately she dreams of none of that, but of a young man, tender and true, with a horse that likes to eat mattresses. He talks to her and listens to her. He kisses her and gathers her kisses. He knows her heart and she knows his. This night Zel goes to bed and dreams of Konrad.

I watch the world. I have no powers anymore. I see as though through a goose eye.

A man on horseback clops southward. He does not come to see the range of colors in the dirt. He is blind. His eyes were scratched beyond sight by a fall into brambles that he knew weren't there as his feet left the tower. He knows who put the brambles there in that crucial instant. The woman called Mother saved his life. So that he could find his love? Or so that he would have to live out his days in the misery of Zel's absence? These questions come to him often, though he has told himself the answer does not matter to him, only to her.

A pigeon rides on his shoulder. The bird sat warbling by the man when he first came to consciousness in the brambles. His hands told him it had a broken wing. It has stayed with the man ever since.

Meta brought the man home. His mother washed the caked blood from his cheeks and eyes. The physicians put poultices and raw eggs and slabs of cold, bloody beef on his wounds. They fought against the darkness in his head; his mother and father prayed against the darkness in his head, but the man accepted it, brushed it aside, even. It was hardly relevant in comparison with what mattered.

They said he needed time to heal. But he crept out and mounted Meta. The menservants brought him back. They took away his clothes so he wouldn't go out again. But he went anyway, naked as a babe. The servants brought him back. They tied him to the bed.

And with time, he healed. But his eyes stayed sightless.

His parents urged him to go forward with his life—forward with his wedding plans. After all, the mystery of the tower begged to be undone, and, not inconsequentially, the young countess was exceedingly wealthy. They pressed hard.

The man would not yield. He called upon his classics

tutor to write a letter on his behalf to the young countess. He laid out what had transpired, detail by detail, each one more strange, more unbelievable, more horrific than the last.

The man did nothing to mitigate those details, knowing full well the impression they gave.

The maiden's father abruptly cut off the betrothal.

The man's parents stood aghast, and silenced, at last.

The man returned to his thoughts, his memories, his true plight.

One day the man thought the bird said, "Who?" The air had cooled by now, and the man knew it was evening. He realized that the moon must by then have gone to nothing and started to grow all over again. The man listened hard. Indeed, the bird said again, "Who?" That's when he first knew for sure the woman was alive.

As soon as his mother would allow him to leave his bed, the man was up and about. He loaded Meta with provisions. Then he left, the pigeon on his shoulder.

They searched the west side of the lake first, but only to confirm what the man suspected: The tower was silent. Deserted. Searching the western slopes revealed no one. So they took to wandering the east side. Eventually horse, man, and bird stumbled their way to the alm with the little wooden footbridge and the high-sided goose nest. It didn't amaze him that in just a few months he could find in his blindness what he had failed to find in two years of sighted searching, for now he had the bird's coos to lead him.

The man entered the cottage and fingered his way around the two rooms, across the two beds, the two chairs at the kitchen table, the two bowls and spoons and plates and cups. The bird plucked at the strings of the fiddle. Meta snuffled at the empty chicken yard. The man slept in the bed and dreamed of a child running on the alm, free and happy, then spirited off to a tower where she could run only in circles. He woke alone and held small, girl, leather shoes in his hands and let his cheek rest on the kitchen table as the sun came in the window. One day he picked up the bedroll to carry it outside, so he could sleep beneath the stars he couldn't see, when he heard something fall soft to the floor. It was a folded paper. Inside were seeds. The man put the seeds in his pocket.

It took till the first snowfall for the man to realize that his love was gone from this home for good. He returned to the castle and passed the first winter there, planning.

In the spring, man, bird, and horse went forth again. They were accompanied by five soldiers. They questioned every worker in the vineyards, every lumberjack, every merchant, every mother. They knelt before little children and spoke in voices they hoped were little. The man gave the children the seeds he'd found under the bedroll. He made them promise to plant them.

As summer came, they traveled beyond the mountains

northward, all the way to a deep sea. The man insisted on camping along the cold shore, on swimming in the cold sea. He dreamed of ice water in thick veins. Of braids impossibly long and brambles springing up from nothing. He cried out in his sleep. At the first snowfall, they rode swiftly south, back to the castle. And the second winter passed.

Spring brought a new plan. The man went forth again accompanied by horse and bird, but now with a small cadre of holy men. They set to buzzing a network of ministers and priests alike across the lands looking for a girl damaged by a witch. The man was tireless. He listened no matter what the language; he sought no matter how far the church; he met maiden after maiden, one more tortured than the last. But none was the maiden who had lived in the tower for two long years. None was his wife.

At last they found themselves in a busy city in a southern river valley. The holy men wanted to return home, where they could serve. But the man wouldn't leave. He dreamed of a little girl coming to market, to a town that seemed to her country eyes as bustling as this big city. Of that girl buying rapunzel and taking it home to feast upon. Of that girl, with so much joy, later joyless and desperate, rocking her head on a stone floor till her jaw almost cracked.

Late, late in December, much later than snow came to the Alps, they headed home. But as they traveled north, they found the roads iced over. They took dangerous risks. The man insisted. When they arrived home at last, the holy men told all. The people looked at each other and rubbed one foot against the other. When the third spring came, no one, no one, was willing to go forth with the man, who had proved himself reckless.

And so, once more, the man headed out into the world with no companions but a bird and a horse. He traveled in an ever-widening spiral, relentlessly.

Konrad's nights are now filled with dreams of a young woman, mysterious and passionate, with words that would drift. She talks to him and listens to him. She kisses him and gathers his kisses. She knows his heart and he knows hers. He wakes every morning refreshed.

Last night a goose honked overhead. Konrad went to sleep and dreamed of Zel's hands on their only night together, moving through the air as if self-propelled, as if they didn't belong to her at all. He felt her gossamer texture.

The day is hot and getting hotter. He doesn't urge Meta to a gallop. They take the road as it comes. His ears gather all.

In the morning the twin girls tug at the woman. "Bird, Maman. Bird."

Zel's heart flutters. She looks out the back window at the goose. The nest is complete, and the goose is busy rolling the painted stones into it. Only three are already in place. It will be a long day for the goose. The tears in Zel's eyes, those tears that almost fell on Mother, well up. But they do not fall. Zel is almost happy.

Zel dresses the girls. They eat. Then they go outside together and sit in the road and wait. The girls talk and giggle.

I listen to the world. I have no powers anymore. I hear as though through a man's ears.

Because Konrad's ears are not filled with the noise of rapid hoofbeats, or perhaps because he remembers the goose honk last night, or maybe because it is simply time at last, he hears the children's laughter even before Zel sees him. And there is something in their shrieks of glee he recognizes. Something of a boy he used to know. Something of a girl he used to know. He laughs out loud.

Zel takes Hélène by one hand, Eve by the other. She walks up the road toward the horse that is Meta. Her feet move more swiftly toward the bird that is Pigeon Pigeon. And now she lets the children's hands go free, for she runs toward the man who is Konrad, the man who dismounts and holds his arms open and runs toward her, surefooted in blindness.

❖

I touch the world. I have no powers anymore. I feel as though with a lover's heart.

Konrad's heart beats slow in this moment, for there is no rush. Now, finally, he has found her, and he has found his children, and there is no rush, for they have all eternity to love one another.

And she is kissing him and he is kissing her and the tears she has held back for five years, the tears that I knew could transform the moment, the tears that had to be saved for the right moment to transform, now come streaming down and drop on the face of the man whose head is cradled in the woman's arms. Zel's tears fall in Konrad's eyes, hot and salty and full of life. He blinks them in, absorbs them; they are now his own tears, and, yes, he can see.

And they see each other and, yes, oh, yes, we are happy.

Donna Jo Napoli teaches linguistics and is the author of several novels for middle graders and young adults, including *The Bravest Thing*; *The Prince of the Pond*; *Jimmy, the Pickpocket of the Palace*; *When the Water Closes Over My Head*; *The Magic Circle* (an ALA Best Book for Young Adults); and, most recently, *Stones in Water*. She lives in Swarthmore, Pennsylvania, with her family.